How he loved a happy ending!

At the altar, old Thom T. Taggart lifted Kit's veil and kissed away the tears of happiness dampening her cheeks. Putting her hand in Boone's, he stepped back to take his place as his grandson's best man.

The minister began to speak. "Dearly beloved, we are gathered here today in the sight of God and this company..."

Thom T. let out a sigh of pure contentment. Things couldn't have turned out better all around if he'd planned it.

Which he had.

Dear Reader,

Friends gave our marriage six months—and who could blame them? My husband-to-be and I couldn't have come from more diverse backgrounds.

He was American Indian-Filipino-Mexican, a Catholic raised primarily in the cosmopolitan Bay Area of San Francisco. I was a true small-town WASP—white Anglo-Saxon Protestant from the Ozark Mountains of Missouri.

We'd only known each other for a few months—and dated for about six weeks—when we decided to get married. Which created a whole new set of problems: he was in the U.S. Marine Corps with orders to one place and I was in the U.S. Navy with orders to another.

Undeterred, we took the plunge, even though not a single member of either family could attend (and the Navy insisted I keep a previously scheduled dental appointment only hours before the wedding). After a weekend honeymoon in Chicago, my new husband reported to his duty station and I reported to mine. For months, we saw each other only on weekends— assuming we could both get liberty.

I never thought we'd look back and laugh, but we have—many times. That rocky beginning was such a small part of our life together. We've been married more than thirty years now; we've lived all over the country, raised a houseful of kids and we've learned what "for richer or poorer, in sickness and in health" really means.

And you know what? Our friends were wrong. This marriage really *will* last "as long as we both shall live."

Sincerely,

Ruth Jean Dale

SHOWDOWN!
Ruth Jean Dale

Harlequin Books

TORONTO • NEW YORK • LONDON
AMSTERDAM • PARIS • SYDNEY • HAMBURG
STOCKHOLM • ATHENS • TOKYO • MILAN
MADRID • WARSAW • BUDAPEST • AUCKLAND

ISBN 0-373-03242-0

Harlequin Romance first edition January 1993

SHOWDOWN!

PROLOGUE

"A TOAST—to Daniel Boone Taggart, the man who has everything."

Standing in the middle of the elegant living room of his New York City penthouse, Boone lifted his crystal champagne glass in a salute to his sister-in-law, Meg, for the toast, and to his brother, Jesse, for his good taste in women. Champagne wasn't Boone's drink; he'd much prefer a lager, but he'd chosen the wine for Meg—who, as it turned out, was in the early stages of pregnancy and sipping orange juice

Beside her, Jesse tossed down the champagne as if eager to get it over with so he could go on to better things. Even wearing a well-tailored dark suit and white shirt, Jesse had the look of the West about him, with his sun-browned skin and the squint of eyes accustomed to wide open spaces.

Boone supposed he himself had lost that cowboy look—knew he had. Years spent in the East, in New York and then London, were not conducive to maintaining a down-home flavor. That was part of the price he'd paid, he thought, twirling the fragile crystal stem between his fingers. He smiled at his sister-in-law. "Nobody's got everything," he objected mildly.

"Maybe not," Meg conceded, "but you come darn close." She ran her gaze around the picture-perfect room, past decorator-designed and -executed surroundings, while ticking off support data: "Rich, young and handsome—a penthouse apartment in Manhattan, a flat in Sloane Square, a partnership in a high-powered international law firm—"

"And fightin' the women off with a stick, I bet," Jesse interjected. "Kinda funny you don't seem happier about it, kid."

"I'm happy," Boone countered, not happy at all to be called "kid" by his older brother. Overlooking a little sibling rivalry, however, he knew he *should* be happy. His life was turning out exactly the way he'd planned. He was in control. He was a success. He knew where he was going.

He liked it that way.

At least, he liked it that way most of the time. Seeing how happy Jesse and Meg were might make him wonder if he was missing anything, but it wasn't enough to make him question his life plan.

Jesse's amused glance seemed to see right through subterfuge. "Whatever you say." He waved his empty glass. "Mind if I help myself?" Without waiting for the acquiescence they both knew was coming, he crossed to the mirrored bar, pulled out a beer, snapped the cap and drank straight from the bottle.

Boone turned to Meg. "So, the two of you are off to Australia. Second honeymoon?"

Meg gave him a nod and a dazzling smile. "Once Randy's little brother or sister appears—" she patted her still-flat middle with satisfaction "—it won't be so easy to get away. Grandfather Randall wanted to take Randy with him to Newport for the summer, anyway, so..."

Jesse came up behind her and slipped his arms around her waist. "If there's one thing we found out the hard way, it's that when opportunity knocks, you better answer 'cause you may not get another chance.''

Meg snuggled back against him. ''Which is why we're here,'' she added. ''By the time we return, you may be gone again, Boone. We wanted to say hi and bye and bring you up to date on the family. A lot's happened in the last year.''

Boone regarded her quizzically. He knew that his grandfather, Thom T., patriarch of the Taggart clan, and Meg's grandfather, John Randall, had masterminded the reunion of Jesse and Meg last summer after a separation that had dragged on for years.

Boone would have bet the outcome of his next case that forcing the estranged couple to spend time alone at the old family homestead near Hell's Bells, Texas, on the pretext of planning their young son's future, would have hastened a divorce, not prevented it.

He'd have been wrong. Meg and Jesse came out a couple again, more in love than ever. So Boone shrugged and said, ''I know all about it.''

''You do?'' Meg looked surprised.

''We've had telephone service between England and Texas for years.''

''But . . . !''

Jesse's arms tightened around his wife and his face took on that mulish expression Boone remembered well from childhood. ''You heard the man, he knows all about it—whatever 'it' is. Tell us, hotshot, when's the last time you talked to Thom T.?''

Boone considered. ''It's been a while,'' he conceded finally. ''We connect when anything important comes up.'' He hesitated. ''So how is Grandpa?''

''Madder'n a wet hen,'' Jesse retorted. ''He wanted us to leave Randy with him while we were gone, but what would he do with an eight-year-old? He seemed to think just because Kit's there—''

"Thank goodness," Meg inserted. "At least he's not alone."

Kit? It took Boone a second to remember the freckle-faced niece of Thom T.'s now-retired housekeeper. It must have been ten years since he'd seen the girl, or even thought about her. Now that he did, it brought a slight smile to his lips. He'd got quite a kick out of teasing the fiery-haired and fiery-tempered little girl.

"She's got a life of her own," Meg continued. "She couldn't spend all her time chasing after Randy."

"I didn't know Kit was back," Boone admitted. "Last I heard she was working in Dallas or Houston or some-place."

Jesse gave a disgusted grunt. "I thought you knew everything. Kit came back for the wedding."

"What wedding?"

"Trey and Rachel's." Meg frowned. "Honestly, Boone, sometimes I don't think you pay enough attention to family affairs."

It took Boone a second to realize she meant Trey Smith and Rachel Cox. He'd known Rachel all her life; she was one of the many recipients of Thom T.'s kindness—in her case, as in many other, a college education. She'd returned to Showdown a few years ago as the town librarian.

Boone had never met Trey Smith, who was apparently some kind of Yankee shirttail relation of the Taggarts. Apparently he'd come to town and swept the redoubtable Ms. Cox off her feet and married her, all within the space of a few months. Knowing how intimidating Rachel could be, Boone figured that must make Trey Smith one hell of a man.

Meg was still talking. "And then Trey got a chance to go to Russia as stunt coordinator on a big film. When the newlyweds left in January, Kit moved back to the ranch— did you know all this? She's the school nurse in Showdown, so the last thing I'd ask her to do with her summer vacation is chase after another kid. Besides, Randy's spent quite a lot of time with Thom T. since we've been fixing up the cabin in Hell's Bells."

"That was a surprise, you two deciding to settle down on that old place way out in the middle of nowhere," Boone admitted. "How's it working out?"

"Great!" Meg and Jesse grinned at each other, and she added, "As long as I can hop a plane and fly off to civilization every so often."

Watching them was a lesson in intimacy for Boone. If ever a couple belonged together, it was these two. Yet they'd married in haste, repented in leisure, and found their way back together only through sheer luck...and a deep and abiding love.

Boone pressed his lips together in a thin line. Being around Jesse and Meg, seeing how much in love they were, made him question his own choices—at least a little. What would he do if one day he realized he'd taken a wrong turn and it was too late to go back?

THE LONGER THEY STAYED, the more melancholy Boone became. He was almost glad when they decided it was time to leave.

Lingering in the marble-floored foyer, Jesse turned to his brother. "Meg and I won't be there for Showdown Days this year, so we're kind of hopin' you can see your way clear to drop in on Thom T. long about then."

"Fourth of July—that's only a few weeks away. I don't know...."

Jesse glowered. "Wouldn't hurt you any to humor the old man. You haven't been home for Showdown Days since that summer you played Sheriff Jack."

Boone's grin was spontaneous. He had indeed played the hero, Sheriff Jack, during the annual week of festivities revolving around the legend of the lawman, the gunman and the Taggarts' great-great-great-aunt Rose. He'd been twenty-one years old, enjoying a last fling before settling down to law school and the life he'd mapped out for himself.

"I got to kiss Marcella Grant," he said, lapsing slightly into the drawl he'd fought long and hard to eradicate from his speech. "Over... and over... and over."

"Bet they'd be glad to let you do it again," Meg teased. "Funny thing is, that gunman—"

Jesse clamped one hand on her elbow. "Let it go, honey. Mr. Know-It-All knows it all, remember?" He reached past her to open the door. "Time to hit the road, amigo," he tossed over his shoulder to his brother.

Meg rose on tiptoe to plant a farewell kiss on Boone's cheek. "Kidding aside, keep an eye on Thom T. for us while we're gone, okay? He misses you."

"I miss him." Boone meant it. "I'll call more frequently, but I don't know if I'll have time to visit before the fall."

"Honestly, Boone." Meg made a face. "You just returned from months and months in London. Surely you rate a little time off."

Boone shrugged. "I suppose so, if I wanted to take it. But I can't just pick up and go at a moment's notice. That's no way to succeed in the Big Apple."

Jesse shook his head, his expression one of disgust. "That is just plain pitiful, little brother. Grandpa's not gettin' any younger."

"Yeah, I know." Boone grasped at straws. "Maybe I can get him to come here."

"Maybe pigs can fly," Jesse scoffed, his usual response to Boone's oft-expressed desire to get their grandfather to come East for a visit—or permanently.

"He'd be better off here with me," Boone argued.

"He's better off where he's happy."

"But he's getting old—he was born in 1908, as he's so fond of reminding us. We've got his health to consider."

Meg stepped between the men, taking her husband's hand firmly. "We've got his *heart* to consider, and that's planted on the Rocking T Ranch in Showdown, Texas. Now will you two stop squabbling like a couple of...brothers!"

BOONE PULLED a beer out of the bar refrigerator and carried it onto the terrace. Leaning against the balcony railing, he stared at the lights sparkling below like a handful of jewels spilled on black velvet. It was the kind of view that inspired poets.

He wasn't a poet; he was an attorney on the fast track. As Meg said, he had everything.

So why did he feel this vague discontent? Gazing out across the city, he relied on logic to reveal the source of his uneasiness.

Must be Thom T., Boone finally concluded. It wasn't right for a man that age to live way out there on the Rocking T, still a working ranch, although on a greatly reduced scale. Mostly the old man's few hired hands played nursemaid to longhorns raised for specialty purposes, and to a small herd of beef cattle under contract to some of the finest restaurants in the country. His grandfather could afford to pay for all the help he needed, sure, but that wasn't the same as relying on kin.

At least Thom T. was no longer alone in the big old Victorian ranch house. Kit... He smiled. She'd come to the ranch as a twelve-year-old, the same year Boone went away to college. Cute little thing. He still remembered the way she'd trailed along after him and Jesse. The summer Boone took part in Showdown Days, she'd also participated, although he couldn't remember in which role. Not a leading one, though.

It had been fun, dressing up in a white hat and strapping on a pair of six-guns. As the hero of the piece, he'd got to ride a white horse and spend a lot of time striking valiant poses while making fairly idiotic speeches. During the week-long tourist extravaganza, he'd even participated in a classic shoot-out on Main Street—the dream of every red-blooded Texas boy!

Funny, the villain of the legend—the man who, if you believed Texas legend, "died in the dirt like a yella dog"—was also named Boone. According to Thom T., "Boone" was an old family name among the Taggarts. But it was a coincidence for which Boone had occasionally spared a passing thought in his younger years.

The telephone rang and the answering machine clicked in before he could reach it. "Daniel, darling, there's going to be a *huuuuge* dinner party Friday night—"

He lifted the receiver. "I'm here, Bree."

"Oh, good. The party's Friday night for the new exec of Borallis and Kleinsweigger. I said we'd *love* to attend—there'll be scads of important people for networking. Good for your career, darling."

"I suppose so, but—"

"No buts. Meet me in half an hour at Trini's for a drink and I promise I'll talk you into it." A series of smacking kiss-sounds and the line went dead.

Boone stood there, realizing again that Bree wanted to pick up where they'd left off when he went to London eighteen months ago. He wasn't sure he wanted that, but he *was* sure he didn't want to go to another damned business dinner.

He wanted to go home to Showdown. He owed it to his grandfather, sure. But the truth was, Boone had never felt as alone as he did now, standing on the brink of the professional success toward which he'd driven himself with single-minded determination for years. Success seemed somehow empty, perhaps because he had no one with whom he wanted to share it.

But if his grandfather moved East . . .

ON HIS RETURN from Trini's two hours later, Boone found another message on his answering machine, this one from a woman whose tone dripped scorn like icicles: "*Mr. Taggart, if it's not too much trouble, your grandfather would like to speak to—*"

A crackle of sound—almost like a tussle for the telephone on the other end—and then Boone instantly recognized the furious Texas drawl of his grandfather, Thom T. Taggart.

"All right, boy, you listen and you listen good. I know you're all tied up in a bunch of tanglement over *high* finance and *big* business, but it's time you hightailed it on home. You hear me? Daniel Boone Taggart, your grandpa's on his deathbed and I ain't just a-woofin'!"

CHAPTER ONE

KIT PROPPED ONE ELBOW on the big walnut table in the middle of the dining room at the Rocking T Ranch. Her rueful glance took in the piles of paper, the colored folders, the bits and pieces of nineteenth-century memorabilia before her.

"If I didn't know better," she remarked, "I'd say this couldn't be done."

Sitting across the table, Rita Lopez straightened, pushing her granny glasses back into place on the bridge of her nose. At thirty-five, Rita was ten years older than Kit, who considered her friend one savvy lady.

Rita's smile looked forced. "Ah, but you *do* know better. Don't quit on me now, Kit. Anybody who can give vaccinations to a roomful of terrified school kids shouldn't have any trouble with this."

"But we've only got a month," Kit pointed out reasonably, "and rehearsals have barely begun."

"Which is just as well, considering that our star eloped day before yesterday with our gunslinger."

"No!" Kit fell back in her chair, realizing why Rita looked so grim. "What happened?"

"Apparently Mary Alice has been sneaking around to meet Junior for weeks—playing the parts of Rose and Boone, the Mysterious Gunslinger, in the Showdown Days pageant was just a front. From what I can gather, her father found out and went lookin' for Junior. So he and

Mary Alice headed for Las Vegas with her daddy in hot pursuit."

"Rita, we are in big trouble!"

Rita nodded. "So what else is new?" She put aside the phony "who's worried?" demeanor. "I knew when Jeannette Cunningham's daughter got sick in Waco we were in for it. I guess when you've chaired Showdown Days as long as Jeannette has, you don't see any need to start early or keep records—so after about 1982 she didn't. This is all we've got to go on." She indicated the litter on the table.

"That's enough," Kit encouraged staunchly. "Remember, everyone in town knows the story."

"Thank heaven. Because if there ever was a complete script, it's lost in the mists of time. A page here, a page there, from umpteen different versions—"

"That's what rehearsals are for, to iron out all the little wrinkles."

"Little wrinkles, she calls it, with cast members dropping like flies." Rita shook her head wearily. "I swear I don't know how Jeannette pulled this thing together every year. It's a nightmare."

"Don't worry, Rita." Kit squeezed her friend's arm sympathetically. "The town's been staging this extravaganza so long we can do it with our eyes closed."

"Thanks for the vote of confidence—I needed that." Rita dug around in the stacks until she found a yellow legal pad and a pencil. "Okay, where are we? Major characters for the pageant—Rose Taggart, the Heroine. We'll have to recast that and the role of Boone the Mysterious Gunfighter. Then we have Jack Guthrie, the Noble Sheriff; James Taggart, the Protective Brother; and his wife, Diana. Right?"

"Right," Kit agreed. "Who's playing Sheriff Jack?"

Rita grimaced. "Bud Williams."

Kit groaned. When she first returned to Showdown last winter, Bud had made a big play for her. All he'd got for his efforts was a cold shoulder. Could he play nobility? She doubted it!

"It gets worse," Rita declared. "I think we're going to have to let Harry Meeks play Boone, the Mysterious you-know-what."

"Tell me you're kidding!"

"Do I look like I'm kidding?" She didn't. "I know he's a bit long in the tooth, but considering the circumstances, we're lucky he's willing to do it."

"I suppose you're right," Kit conceded without her usual spirit. "Who else?"

"Lee Cox is James Taggart—"

"Good. That's good."

"And Jenny Merton's niece, Chelsea, who's visiting for the summer from California, will play James's wife, Diana."

They sat in silence for a moment, and then Kit asked the obvious question. "What about Rose?"

Rita sighed. "Heaven only knows. I've called an emergency meeting of the Showdown Days Committee to discuss it. We'll have to do something quick, even if we do it wrong."

That, Kit knew, was the truth; Miss Rose Taggart was the unofficial queen of Showdown Days, and all eyes would be on her. Once upon a time, Kit had dreamed of playing the part herself, but that was no more than a childhood fantasy.

To begin with, she wasn't a native of Showdown, or even a native Texan if anyone cared to get technical about it. It was just that she loved the town and the state so much that she tried to pretend she'd been born here like most everyone else. "Who's in the running?" she asked.

"My lips are sealed." Rita graphically demonstrated, then relented. "All I can say is that the committee will pick the prettiest, the sweetest, the most *Southern* Southern belle in all of Showdown to play the fabled Miss Rose Taggart—assuming she's also a quick study and has the guts of a train robber. Because that's what it'll take to pull this off on such short notice."

Put that way, it sounded pretty scary. But to encourage Rita, Kit shoved doubts aside. "You'll think of someone," she declared.

"Thanks, but unfortunately, that's not our only problem."

"More bad news?" Kit sifted through papers, looking for anything that might resemble a script. She pulled out a sheet that began in midsentence: " . . . riding a magnificent black stallion down the middle of Main Street, wearing twin six-shooters with pearl handles and ten notches in each . . ."

"It never rains but it pours," Rita said glumly. "You know the wedding dress that's been used for every pageant since 1961?"

"Sure." Kit held on to the lone page of script and rummaged around for more. "What about it?"

"It's in tatters, that's what about it." Rita's dark eyes flashed. "I knew last year the Cooper girl wasn't a size eight, but she swore she was. Practically every seam in that dress is strained to the breaking point—or beyond."

"So what are you going to do?"

Rita shrugged. "What can we do? Dig up another dress. Maybe we can find one in an attic. Otherwise, somebody will have to make a new one—and it won't be me! With the kids home for summer vacation, it's all I can do to try and pull this confounded celebration together without taking that on, too. Compared to this, teaching a passel of rambunctious curtain climbers is a stroll in the park.''

"Well, don't look at me!" Kit said, aghast. "I can't sew. I can operate for hangnails but I can't sew. Want a tetanus shot? That I can do. I can read a doctor's handwriting—there's a skill you may need. But I can't sew.''

"Are you trying to tell me you can't sew?" Rita laughed. "Don't worry about it. I've got plenty lined up that you *can* do. We've got enough problems to go a—'' The irritated tinkle of a small bell interrupted.

"—round.'' She glanced toward the door leading to the rear of the big old Victorian ranch house. "Sounds like Thom T.'s on the warpath. That's the third time he's rung that bell in the last fifteen minutes. He's a testy old gent when he's well and a real bobcat when he's not.''

"You'd be testy, too, if you had an ungrateful grandson who wouldn't even come home for a family emergency.'' Kit rose along with her temper. "We left a message on his answering machine last night, and he didn't even return the call.''

"Back to bad-mouthing Boone, I see.'' Rita grinned. "How about Jesse and Meg? They coming?''

Kit shook her head. "Thom T. wouldn't let me call them. They're on their way to Australia for a second honeymoon.'' She hesitated, feeling unaccountably melancholy. "She's pregnant again. They're both really excited.''

Rita leaned forward to pat Kit's hand. "You don't look too pleased about it, honey.''

"Oh, I am!'' It was true; Kit was thrilled for Jesse, whom she regarded as a brother, and his wife, whom she didn't know as well but liked immensely. "It's just that it makes me realize how much I'm missing...."

"Kit! Dad-blast it, girl, if you don't get in here I'm a-gettin' up and this time I mean it!"

Kit and Rita exchanged tolerant glances. Everyone in Showdown knew and understood Thom T. Taggart's penchant for drama. In fact, they took a certain civic pride in his many eccentricities.

Hurrying to the old man's assistance, Kit heard the sound of an automobile driving into the ranch yard, but she didn't turn back. Somebody else coming to brave Thom T.'s temper, she supposed. There'd been a constant stream of visitors since the accident. None seemed able to influence his disposition for the better, however.

Poor Thom T.! He'd been prickly as a cactus pear ever since that crazy black horse had thrown him, breaking his leg, two days ago. He'd put a lot of time into that animal. Kit knew he felt thoroughly humiliated at being bested, although heaven knew that at his age he shouldn't have been anywhere near an outlaw horse.

Failure to reach his youngest grandson on the phone the other night hadn't done a lot for Thom T.'s disposition, either. "Dad-gummed irresponsible sprout," he'd groused when he hung up the receiver. Ungraciously he'd allowed Kit to adjust the pillow beneath his cast. "That New York was bad enough, but London! It's done corrupted him for sure."

She'd been patient with the old man—not that it was difficult. She prided herself on being patient with *all* her patients. With Thom T., though, it was more than the professional response of a registered nurse be-cause...because she loved him. She'd never had a father, nor even a father figure, until she'd come to live in this big old wood-frame house. She'd been twelve years old, and Thom T. Taggart was the first man she'd ever trusted enough to love.

His grandson Boone was the second—and what a disappointment *he* turned out to be.

So I'm batting .500, she thought wryly; *that's not so bad.* She knocked lightly on the octogenarian's door, then entered. "Need something?" she asked cheerfully.

"Naw." Thom T.'s tight mouth turned down in a sarcastic curve. "I just enjoy yellin' to hear my head rattle. Of course I need somethin'!"

Thom T. lay in a hospital bed specially installed for him, his upper body raised and braced on his bent arms. Wiry and rawhide-tough, he still boasted a head of thick silver hair constantly standing on end—kind of like a mad cowboy scientist, Kit often thought with private amusement.

Waking to the bed, she smoothed the sheets while waiting for him to get to the point. When he didn't, she ventured a guess. "If you're in pain..."

"I ain't in no pain." He collapsed back on the bed, clearly disgruntled. Then he heaved a gusty sigh and reached out awkwardly to pat her hand. "You're a good girl, Kitty. Don't know how you put up with a cantankerous old goat like myself."

That was too close to an apology for comfort. Kit turned her hand beneath his until she could squeeze his gnarled fingers. It wasn't like him to show any sort of vulnerability and the fact that he did so now made her uneasy. "Thom T., you know I—"

"All I know for sure's that Father Time's catchin' up to me and I might as well admit it." He shook his head tiredly. "One a' these fine days I'm gonna have to face the fact I'm not the man I once was. What'll happen to the Rockin' T when that time comes?"

With her free hand, Kit dragged a chair close to the bed and sat down without releasing her grip on him. "That time's a long way off," she said, her voice trembling. She cleared her throat and went on. "The Rocking T's always been run by Taggarts. It'll always be here."

"Yep, but I won't."

"Thom T.!" Was he trying to tell her that he didn't expect to recover? No! Her hand squeezed his so hard he squawked a protest. "Don't talk like that!" she cried. "You're doing great—Dr. Preston said so. You can't expect the recuperative powers of a teenager, but you *will* get well."

"I know it." He looked incensed. "I ain't near ready to kick the bucket yet."

She sagged in relief. "Then what...?"

"Use your head, gal." He spoke condescendingly, as if she were still a child; compared to him, just about *everybody* was a child. "I cain't go on forever, agreed?"

"Well, sure. Nobody can go on forever." It pained her to admit his mortality, even in the abstract.

"When I go, who'll want the Rockin' T? Who'll even care what happens to it?"

I will, she cried silently, *and not because of any monetary value. It's the only real home I've ever had. Here I received the only love I could ever count on.*

But she wasn't a Taggart and she wasn't a fortune hunter, so she said tentatively, "Jesse..."

"Jesse's started his own spread on the old home place. He don't want the Rockin' T no more."

Kit's shoulder slumped. "You've got two grandsons. If Jesse isn't interested, maybe Boone..." Her brave words trailed off in defeat.

"Yep, and maybe pigs can fly." He pulled his hand free of her death grip and grinned, the first honest amusement she'd seen in him since the accident. "Well, maybe they can! I figure when the chips are down, ol' Boone may surprise us all."

"Let us pray," Kit murmured without hope.

"What's that?"

"As you say." She stood up, longing to lean over and kiss his cheek. But that wasn't the kind of thing she'd ever done before, and she feared he'd be somehow offended. "Would you like me to read to you for a while?"

"Naw. I know that good-lookin' Señora Lopez is down there waitin' for you."

"But you must have called me for a reason," Kit protested.

"Yep, but I kinda forget now what it was." He gave her a sheepish look.

"You're sure?" She tucked the sheet around him. "Would you like something to drink before I go? Water? Juice?"

Deliberately she didn't mention coffee; the man drank far too much of it, and every cup loaded with caffeine— "I don't know how anybody can choke down that unleaded stuff," he'd say when she pushed decaffeinated coffee at him.

"No, I don't want a drink—not less'n it's bourbon and branch," he said, growing testy once more. "I want—"

"A little company?"

A chill struck Kit between the shoulder blades and raced in both directions. She'd know that voice anywhere, even with words couched in accents harsh and unnatural to her ears. She stood stock-still, seeing the pure and painful relief wash over the old man's face.

"Boone," Thom T. said in a voice little more than a satisfied grunt. His bony fingers crushed the sheet. "You came."

Kit couldn't stand the naked vulnerability in the old man's expression. She turned around, her movements jerky and uncoordinated. And sure as the world, there was Daniel Boone Taggart, tall and broad-shouldered and absolutely gorgeous.

He wasn't supposed to be here—she hadn't had time to prepare. Rattled, all she could do was scowl at him. He didn't seem to notice. Brushing past her with only a quick nod of acknowledgment, he stepped to the bedside and looked down at his grandfather. "You old reprobate," he said. "Who was it used to tell me that there's nary a horse that can't be rode, and nary a rider that can't be throwed?"

A wide grin split Thom T.'s face. "You young whippersnapper," he goaded in mock fury. "It was me!"

For a moment Kit thought Boone would take the old man in his arms, but then he simply grasped Thom T. forearm to forearm, hand to elbow. Swallowing the lump in her throat, she walked out of the room and closed the door behind her.

Why should seeing Boone again after all these years leave her so shaken?

Rita waited in the hall, a broad smile on her face. "That's just the medicine Thom T. needs," she predicted with satisfaction. "Gosh, doesn't Boone look great?"

Kit gave a haughty sniff. "I didn't notice," she lied.

"Sure you did." Rita took Kit's arm and steered her down the hall toward the dining room, where all their files and papers still littered the table. "You may be mad at him, but you're not blind! Now, let's get back to business and figure out how to keep Showdown Days from collapsing around our ears."

The two women worked a while longer, but it soon became apparent to Kit that she was too distracted to concentrate. She kept listening for sounds from Thom T.'s bedroom and occasionally heard some—once a shout of laughter from both men, then a shout of outrage from Thom T.

Time passed and twinges of jealousy turned into outright pangs. Kit found herself gritting her teeth and glancing toward the hallway again and again. After nearly an hour of this, Rita began to gather up her materials and put them back into boxes.

"I guess we've done about all we can for today," she said.

"What?" Kit stared guiltily. "But we've hardly done anything."

"Honey, as agitated as you are, I can work faster alone," Rita said bluntly.

"I—I'm sorry," Kit stammered. "It's just…you should have seen his face, Rita."

"Whose face? I saw Boone's and found it extraordinarily attractive." She winked for salacious effect.

"Not Boone's! Thom T.'s." Kit picked up a cardboard box and followed Rita through the door, out of air-conditioning into a blast of June heat. "He's pinned all his hopes on Boone, now that Jesse and Meg are together again and have gone off on their own."

Rita hefted the box into her pickup truck. "I thought Thom T. liked Meg."

"He does." Kit deposited her box beside the other. "In fact, he was instrumental in getting them back together. I think, now that they are, he doesn't want to be a burden."

"In that case, what's wrong with counting on Boone? He's a Taggart, too."

Kit pursed her lips, remembering the smooth Easterner who'd walked into the sickroom. "You'd never know it to look at him—or listen to him, for that matter."

"I thought he looked and sounded plenty good." Rita moved her eyebrows up and down in a credible imitation of Groucho Marx. She threw open the driver's door and climbed into the cab of the truck. "Think you could stand a word of advice from someone older and arguably wiser?"

Kit groaned, "Must I?"

"You must." Rita slammed the door and leaned out through the open window. "What we've got here is the dreaded equal-but-opposite reaction."

"You've lost me."

"No, I haven't. When you were fifteen, you fell for Boone Taggart like a ton of bricks—no, don't deny it. I was there. I saw you mooning after him when he played the hero in Showdown Days."

Kit felt her cheeks burn with mortification. "That was a silly crush," she said stiffly. "It has nothing to do with now."

"It has *everything* to do with now, because nothing he's done since has been right in your eyes. I think you took his rejection of you as a rejection of Thom T. and the Rocking T and Texas and the whole enchilada."

"Well? Isn't that how it's turned out?"

"No, it's not how it's turned out. Because you were wrong in the first place—Boone never rejected you."

"Funny, it sure felt like rejection."

Rita reached through the open window and patted Kit's shoulder, her dark eyes filled with sympathy. "Honey, he didn't reject you, because *he never even knew you were alive.* You were a child and he was a young man of twenty-one. Give him another chance, will you?"

She started the engine and eased the truck into gear.
"Don't forget, full committee meeting Thursday at six at
the community building."

With a cheery wave, Rita drove away, leaving Kit
standing there, fuming in the dust. She was banging pots
and pans in the kitchen—still fuming—when Boone found
her a half hour later.

When he walked in, she gave him an unfriendly glance.
"So, what do you think?" she demanded, nodding in the
general direction of Thom T.'s room.

Boone seemed unperturbed by her rudeness. "I think
he may be down but he's a long way from out. He's the
same cantankerous old coot he's always been." The af-
fectionate tone took the sting from his words.

"He's missed you."

"I've missed him."

"Have you?" She slammed down the skillet and faced
him, hands on hips.

He looked her over, his blue-gray eyes narrowing. She
looked him over right back, something she hadn't been
able to do in the first shock of seeing him. Her initial impression increased her dismay. Where had the good ol'
Texas cowboy gone?

The man before her could never be mistaken for anything but what he was: a high-powered big-city dude. She
ran her disdainful gaze over him, trying to cultivate contempt for his expensive sportswear, expensive haircut—
make that hair*style*, she corrected herself—expensive
leather sneakers, expensive *everything*. In local parlance,
he looked like he just stepped out of a bandbox.

Oh, but he was just as handsome as she remembered,
maybe more. His face was as lean and attractive as ever,
but she saw a jaded expression there now, as if he no
longer fully believed in much of anything. The straight

nose and generous mouth were the same, but the effect was different without the ready smile she remembered.

He walked to the small worktable in the middle of the room and sat down on a stool, his movements easy and self-assured. He seemed taller than she'd thought, and it shocked her to realize he might even be an inch or two more than Jesse's six one.

Boone folded his arms on the table and leaned forward, biceps bulging beneath the short-sleeved blue polo shirt. Big-city living hadn't made him soft, she admitted to herself. He probably kept his body in shape by visits to some health club, not by honest labor.

"All right, tell me what I did," he ordered. "It must have been awful."

Embarrassment burned her cheeks and she turned away. Rudeness had never been her forte. "I'm sure I don't know what you're talking about," she denied haughtily, adding, "but you might have warned us you were coming!"

"Warned you? I wasn't aware that it was necessary to warn anybody before I came home."

His nonchalant use of the word "home" stopped her for a moment. Although she said nothing, he picked up on her reaction, for he went on easily, "Yes, home. I grew up here. It'll always be home, no matter how far away I go or how infrequently I return."

Could that mean . . . ? She stared at him, trying to read a deeper significance into his words. The man should have been a professional poker player, for he gave nothing away, nothing at all. He'd always been more self-contained than Jesse, but he'd *really* turned into a cool customer.

He didn't smile; he didn't frown. He simply regarded her with...indifference, she supposed. Then he smiled and she was lost.

"I was surprised when Jesse and Meg told me you were back," he said, "surprised and pleased. I'm glad Thom T. wasn't alone when it happened."

"I'm glad you're glad," she said, surrendering to sarcasm.

He didn't rise to the bait or react in any way. "I hear you're a nurse."

"That's right."

"Lucky for Thom T."

"Not lucky. He put me through school. I owe him more than I can ever—" She stopped short, not trusting him enough to reveal her deepest feelings. "He's family," she said in a tight voice.

A slight frown touched Boone's face but that was all.

Kit opened the refrigerator door and peered inside. "Will you be here for supper?" She'd planned a light meal for herself and her patient, but...

"Yes, and breakfast, too. Where's Elva?"

Kit swallowed hard. *He was staying, at least for a while.* What had he asked? About Thom T.'s housekeeper? "Sh-she wanted time off this summer to spend with her grandchildren in Colorado, so I'm holding the fort. She'll be back in September." Kit took the chicken from the refrigerator and stood there holding it uncertainly.

"You're free to do that?" His strong brows rose, drawing her attention to his eyes. They were the most intriguing shade of blue-gray with long sooty lashes slightly darker than his hair.

What was the matter with her? He was waiting for an answer. "I'm the school nurse in Showdown, so my summer's my own, more or less," she said. "I help Doc Preston out a few mornings a week at the clinic, so I've got time." She cast him an accusing glance. "Besides, I *like* being with Thom T."

She fully expected him to retort, "Meaning I don't?" Then they could get everything out in the open as she longed to do. She'd seen this confrontation coming ever since Thom T. had broken his leg; she had all her words of accusation neatly lined up, ready to hurl at him.

But Boone surprised her yet again.

"That's great," he said. "He's fond of you, too." He stood up and stretched luxuriously. His knit shirt expanded to the bursting point across his muscled chest before he lowered his arms with a sigh. "I think I'll go unpack," he said. "I put my bags in my old room."

"You *what?*" His old room was next to Jesse's, which was now her room.

"Got a problem with that?"

He looked amused. How dared he look amused! "No," she said stiffly. "No, of course not. How...how long will you be staying?"

"Only long enough to convince Thom T. to sell this place and move back East with me." He gave her a brilliant smile. "Call me when dinner's ready.

Whistling, he strode from the room.

CHAPTER TWO

KIT WORRIED about Boone's pronouncement while she broiled the chicken. What kind of man would sell his birthright and break his grandfather's heart?

She'd confront him, that's what she'd do. Ripping salad greens into a bowl, she vowed to force a showdown at the first opportunity—but when might that be?

Boone didn't appear again until she called him for supper. She'd set up a card table in Thom T.'s big bedroom at the old man's insistence, so they could eat together. The very idea of sharing the meal with Boone took away her appetite, because she knew she couldn't challenge his insensitivity with his grandfather present.

Then Boone walked into the bedroom, and she dropped the salad forks and had to go get more. Despite the gloss of civilization, he had lost none of his attractiveness. Maintaining this state of constant wariness when he was around was already beginning to wear her down.

The food tasted like hay in her mouth, but the two men ate with gusto, especially Thom T. He'd been "off his feed," as he said, since the accident. He seemed intent on making up for it tonight.

The reason for his revived spirts was painfully obvious to Kit. Every time he looked at his grandson, Thom T. positively glowed. And Boone...Boone seemed completely comfortable and at ease.

He wasn't, though. At least not as much as he let on, Kit decided. If he were, he'd relax back into the speech patterns and accent of his youth. He never did. His diction, his mid-Atlantic television-newscaster accent, never varied.

You'd think he'd never heard a Texas drawl in his life; you'd think he'd been born in a palace. Well, he didn't fool her! And he wouldn't fool his grandfather much longer, either, not if he went through with his dastardly plan—

"*Kit!*"

She blinked in confusion. Thom T. was glowering at her. "I'm sorry," she said, hopelessly lost. "What did you—?"

"I *said*," Thom T. hollered, "Doc promised I'd be up and around in the flick of a drake's tail. Ain't that right!"

Somehow it seemed that if she softened toward the old man in front of Boone, she'd reveal a weakness Boone could use against her. Even so, she couldn't stop the smile spreading across her face. Truth was, she just plain felt more comfortable smiling, especially at Thom T. "He didn't exactly promise," she hedged. "He did say that for a man your age—"

"Baloney! I'm every bit as much man as I ever was." But he winked one eye and gave a cackle of laughter. "Pert near, anyway."

"Just what *did* the doctor say?" Boone asked Kit later. He'd followed her and the dirty dishes down to the kitchen and was leaning against the refrigerator, watching her bustle around.

His long supple body and bland expression reminded her of a jungle cat in a tabby-cat suit. "That he's doing very well, but old bones take longer to knit." She busied herself scraping plates and loading them into the dishwasher.

"Was it . . ." Boone hesitated and looked away, for all the world as if to conceal his feelings. After a moment he glanced back, expression calm and unruffled. "Was it a bad break?"

He's sincerely worried about his grandfather, Kit realized with surprise. Why had he felt it necessary to hide his concern?

"Fairly bad," she admitted. "Of course, any break at his age is a bad break." She spoke gently, all her instincts and training to protect and support surging to the fore.

Boone sighed. "I've got to get him out of here before he kills himself." His glance held steady with hers, as if he knew she'd been waiting to pounce on him and had decided a good offense was the best defense. He'd obviously chosen his battleground, and it was here and now.

She'd been ambushed. Kit tried to fight her dismay by reminding herself that *she* had intended to bring up the subject. She took a deep breath. "You're wrong. Giving up the Rocking T would kill him."

He shook his head with deliberate slowness. "You're being melodramatic. You said yourself he's not as young as he used to be."

"Who is?" Distraught, she ran a hand through her mane of wildly curling hair. Coppery tendrils escaped, springing forward to tickle her cheeks. "Age doesn't always mean diminished capacity, Boone."

"It does, Kit. At least, diminished *physical* capacity. You said it yourself—old bones."

She slammed the dishwasher door closed. "Don't try to turn my own words back on me. You talk like a lawyer!"

"Wonder why?" His brows rose in exaggerated astonishment. "Let's look at this calmly and logically. It's not safe for him to live alone any longer."

"Alone? Alone! What am I, the invisible woman?" She whirled around to punch viciously at the dishwasher buttons. The machine roared into action.

The angrier and more alarmed she became, the calmer and more controlled he appeared. "Take it easy," he soothed. "We're on the same side, remember?" He might have used an identical tone to calm a hysterical client. "I thank God you were here when he needed you, but—"

"No buts. I'll always be here when he needs me," she vowed, standing rigid as a spear.

"Kitty, Kitty." He shook his head and gave her a smile she took as condescending. "You know that's impossible. You'll get a better job and move away eventually."

His use of her childhood nickname threw her momentarily, but she plunged ahead, "I turned down a better job to come here," she informed him.

He dipped his head in minute concession. "Even so, you'll have other opportunities. And one of these days you'll meet some lucky man and get married. Have you thought about that?"

"Don't you dare condescend to me, Daniel Boone Taggart!" She stood rooted to the spot by indignation. "Don't you understand what this place means to your grandpa? His ancestors fought and died for it. *Your* ancestors fought and died for it."

A faint grimace that might have been a smile tugged at his mouth. "I know. Taggarts fought at the Alamo, fought Comanches, and fought at the drop of a hat."

"Well, they *did!* And you should be..." She paused long enough to draw a deep breath and steady the waver in her voice. She wanted to say, "You should be horse-whipped!" but instead said, "You should be proud of them."

"What makes you so sure I'm not?" He tilted his head and looked at her with cool superiority.

"Oh, Boone!" She wrung her hands, so disappointed she felt like crying. This was even worse than she had anticipated. This man... She spoke her thoughts out loud. "Don't you have any heart left at all? If you did, you'd see that family is the most precious thing in the world."

A faint tinge of color darkened his high cheekbones, but he gave no other indication that her words might sting. "Be reasonable, Kit. Thom T. obviously can't be trusted to know his own limitations. Because I care for him, I've got to get him out of here before he does himself real harm."

"It would kill him to hear you say that," she whispered. She felt completely helpless. How could she deal with this stranger, this man of ice?

For an instant she thought she saw his expression soften, but then he straightened and shrugged. "You're wrong. He's a tough old bird—just not tough enough to be taming wild horses. I'm taking him out of here for his own good, Kitty, but I'll admit it's for my good, too. I want him near me, where I can take care of him if—make that *when*—he needs me. Despite what you may think, I love my grandfather."

He took two steps toward the door and stopped to slant her a cool glance. "Family does count with me, Kitty. Why don't you make it easier on all of us by staying out of this?"

Kit had never been more firmly put in her place. She was an outsider; as such, her opinion didn't matter.

There seemed nothing left for her to say. She stood there dumbly and watched him walk out of the kitchen.

He didn't hurry and he didn't dawdle. Obviously her plea meant nothing to him, made no impression whatsoever.

She couldn't believe it.

Deep in her heart, she'd thought she meant more to the Taggarts than that.

BOONE PAUSED outside his grandfather's door to smooth the frown from his face. Kit was going to be a problem. Her antipathy surprised him, to say the least.

She'd always been passionate in her attitudes and causes, he remembered; she'd never done anything by half measures. Obviously she cared very much for Thom T., but the ultimate responsibility wasn't hers, it was Boone's and Jesse's.

She'd marry one of these days, have children, and then those nurturing instincts would find another outlet. She was young—in her mid-twenties—and pretty.... He smiled, remembering the way her big bright smile crinkled the corners of her eyes, and that wild mane of red hair fought restraint as if it had a will of its own.

A multitude of amber freckles still peppered her fair skin; he remembered how she'd always hated them. He'd kind of liked them, himself, thinking they gave her a certain cachet that belonged with coppery hair and clear green eyes.

They'd gotten along very well in the old days. What the hell was wrong with her now? Did she seriously think he'd ever do anything that would hurt his grandfather? The frown threatened to return; Boone slipped on a smile and opened the bedroom door.

Kit McCrae wasn't blood kin. They'd both do well to remember that.

BOONE CAME DOWN to breakfast the next morning all decked out like a dude. Kit, putting the finishing touches on Thom T.'s tray of oatmeal and stewed prunes, could hardly conceal her contempt for his neat slacks, yellow polo shirt and sparkling white leather cross-trainers.

He gave her a nod that could have been friendly but probably wasn't and helped himself to a cup of coffee. "Some things never change," he said.

"What?" Surprised, she glanced up, managing to drip prune juice on the pristine white place mat.

He nodded at the tray. "Thom T.'s breakfast. Summer, winter, spring and fall—oatmeal and prunes."

Something in his voice implied criticism, but she bit back a retort. She had to stay—get?—on his good side. She'd lain awake half the night deciding on the best course of action, and that was it—bite her tongue and butter him up. Which meant controlling her unpredictable temper.

She reached for a mug. "Boone..." she began in a wheedling tone.

Another man might have groaned. This man just looked up from his cup and waited for her to go on— which made her want to groan herself.

"About Thom T.'s accident... It wasn't what you think."

His brows rose. "What do I think?"

"Probably that he—I mean, that Thom T. must have—" She was starting to babble, stumbling over her own sincerity. Guarding her words had never been her style, but she simply had to calm down. "I'm sure you thought he just fell off some old plug because he's too old to be messin' with horses at all. You couldn't be more wrong."

An almost smile tugged at his mouth again. "That's not what I thought, but just for the sake of argument, do go on."

"Oh...okay." She hesitated a moment, chewing at her lower lip. "See, the horse that did it isn't just any old horse—he's a really magnificent animal. Before he came here, he'd been misused pretty badly at a ranch down south. Nobody could ride him and he'd got a reputation as one tough outlaw."

"That's the horse my eighty-something grandpa tried to ride?" Boone shook his head in apparent disbelief. "Kitty, you're not making a strong case here for Thom T.'s competence."

"I would if you'd let me finish," she flashed before she could stop herself.

"Be my guest." He crossed his arms, biceps bulging beneath the knit. He didn't look angry or offended— amused, maybe.

"Thom T. spent hours, days, weeks working with that black horse. We all thought he was really making headway. He had that horse to the point where he could throw on the saddle and lead him around, no problem. Even so, Bud Williams insisted on being first to crawl on board, just to iron out any kinks."

"Obviously something went wrong."

Kit felt the muscles in her jaw tighten at his condescending tone. "Thom T. got the horse all ready, but Bud was late getting here. Thom T. didn't much...like the idea of someone else riding the Outlaw, anyway, so—"

"You don't have to go on. I get the picture."

She didn't *want* to go on, but felt she had to. "No you don't! Thom T. had every reason to think he'd gentled that horse."

"Obviously he was wrong." A muscle jumped in Boone's jaw. "Anybody ridden the animal since?"

"Well...." She looked away. "No, but—"

"Anybody *tried?*"

"Yes!" She glared at him across the breakfast bar. "Bud did. And a...a couple of Thom T.'s other ranch hands, but—"

"Give it up, Kitty. You're only convincing me that I was right in my previous assessment." His cool blue-gray eyes held level.

As if he needed convincing! Kit thrust out her lower lip in resentment. "But you're *not* right! Thom T. doesn't deserve to be put out to pasture because he made one mistake. And that Outlaw horse doesn't deserve a trip to the glue factory because nobody around here is man enough to ride him!"

The corners of Boone's eyes crinkled and his lips twitched as if only through a mighty effort did he manage to sidestep a genuine smile. Sounding amused, he said, "Now isn't that a relief, yelling instead of trying to do a snow job on me?"

"It wasn't a snow job. It was my vain attempt to get you to listen to reason," she said with dignity.

At last his grin broke free, wide and dazzling. "At least you tried. Where is this renegade animal at the moment?"

"In the far corral, waiting for Bud to come get him."

"Bud?" Boone curved strong brown fingers around his coffee mug. "Why?"

"To take him back to the Box W."

"For what purpose?"

"For *riding* purposes." Kit fidgeted with the tray of food rapidly cooling beneath the onslaught of air-conditioning. "After Thom T.'s accident, everybody and his brother tried to ride that horse, and every blasted one of 'em got tossed. Bud thinks if he's got a few days to work with old Outlaw without interference—"

"No."

She blinked. "No what?"

"No, Bud's not taking the horse."

"B-but somebody's got to do it." She frowned uncertainly. "Outlaw's getting wilder by the day. Every time he throws somebody else it makes him that much more determined to get the next one."

"Why not send him to Jesse?"

"Because Jesse's out of the country and will be for who knows how long. If that black hellion runs wild until then, we may as well forget it. Somebody's got to break him in sooner than that or it'll never get done."

Boone's expression grew, if anything, colder still. "I know Bud Williams, and he's hell on women and horses. I wouldn't let him touch anything I valued."

"Then who's going to do it? You?"

The scornful words were out before Kit could stop them. She gasped and clapped one hand over her mouth in disbelief that she should have said such a thing—and to Boone! Boone was—make that *had once been*—every bit as fine a rider as Jesse. And Jesse had gone on the professional rodeo circuit and become a world champion.

A dark flush covered Boone's lean cheeks and his eyes narrowed to angry slits—the first real show of anger she'd got from him. She braced herself for a verbal assault, but he merely shrugged.

"Katherine McCrae, it occurs to me that you and I have a few things to get straight here," he said in a pleasant tone. "You seem to be laboring under the misapprehension that—"

The telephone on the wall shrilled, and Kit jumped a
foot. *Saved by the bell, for the moment at least.* She
snatched up the receiver and choked out, "Rocking T.
This is Kit—may I help you?" Her anxious gaze never left
Boone.

"Oh, hello," came the surprised voice of a woman. A
young surprised voice. "Is this the Taggart ranch in
Showdown, Texas?"

"That's right." Kit watched Boone from beneath lowered lashes. My gosh but he was a cool customer! She'd
all but called him a—

Lilting laughter, and the woman said, "Then this is the
right number. May I speak to Daniel Taggart, please? Tell
him it's Bree calling."

Daniel? Nobody had ever called Daniel Boone Taggart
by his first name—not around here, anyway. Kit gave him
a saccharine smile. "It's for you, *Daniel,*" she announced, trying valiantly to keep her lip from curling.
"It's *Bree.*"

Picking up the breakfast tray, she marched from the
room. Behind her, she could hear Boone saying, "I don't
know how long I'll be, Bree. It depends on what the doctor tells me. . . ."

BUD WILLIAMS DROVE into the ranch yard at midmorn-
ing, his pickup truck pulling a two-horse trailer. With a
nervous glance around for Boone, Kit walked out to meet
him.

She hadn't remembered that Boone and Bud knew each
other, but if she'd given it a thought, she would have.
They were the same age—thirty-one—and had grown up
in the same small town attending the same small school.

Boone was obviously less than impressed with Bud, and
in all honesty, Kit could see why. Bud was a good ol' boy,
long on bravado and short on sensitivity. He'd married

right out of high school, but that union had dissolved five years ago after three kids. As Kit recalled, the ex-wife had remarried and taken the children to Florida.

Bud braked in a cloud of dust and waved. Kit waved back, then peered into the cab of the truck. Sure enough, Bud had brought help in the form of his twin sister, appropriately called Sissy. She and Kit had known each other casually for years.

Sissy bounded out of the truck. "Howdy, yawl," she greeted, brushing off the seat of her jeans. "Bud thought he might need help with that Outlaw horse, so he brought reinforcements and I'm them."

"Looks like you made the trip for nothing." Kit turned to Bud, who stood beside the truck shaking out a loop in his lariat. "Boone's here and he says—"

"I'll tell him, Kit."

Boone's voice, coming so unexpectedly from behind her, made Kit jump. He seemed to have a downright talent for that.

The two men shook hands, the ritual a shade short of cordial.

Sissy's eyes sparkled with interest. "Boone Taggart, as I live and breath—come give me a hug, stranger!"

Sissy held out her arms and Kit watched curiously to see how the cool Mr. Boone Taggart would handle such familiarity. To her surprise, he seemed perfectly delighted to give Sissy a friendly hug—maybe more than friendly.

Kit tossed her head and whirled about to follow Bud to the corral.

Bud opened the gate a smidgen and stepped inside, his attention focused on the black stallion eyeing him from across the hard-packed earth of the enclosure. He shook out his loop and took a step to one side, to get the snubbing post in the center out of his line of vision. The trembling Outlaw pawed the ground, his nostrils flaring.

"Not so fast, Williams."

Boone's voice cracked like a bullwhip, and Kit's jaw tightened in response. Sissy followed at Boone's heels, her expression one of awe—and fascination.

"What's the problem?" Bud demanded pettishly. "Stand back while I show this hoss who's boss." Again he started forward, the loop trailing on the ground behind him.

Boone stepped neatly onto the rope, bringing the other man up short. "What in the hell?" Bud swung around, saw Boone's hard face, and his own reddened.

Boone's smile was not pleasant but his voice was. "We've had a little change of plans, that's all. The Outlaw stays here."

"But...damn it, man, Thom T....that Outlaw..." Bud sputtered and jerked his head toward the disputed animal. "Somebody's gotta show that hoss who's boss."

Boone shoved his hands deep into his trouser pockets and rocked back on his heels. "I want the horse left here."

"What for?" Bud demanded plaintively. "It's not like *you're* gonna ride him!" He guffawed and began to coil his rope, muttering and swearing under his breath.

Kit stiffened with shock. The Boone she knew—*any* Taggart she knew—would wipe up the floor with any man who suggested there was anything on four legs he couldn't handle. Without moving a muscle, Boone seemed to strain forward; an expression almost of longing crossed his face. For a moment there, Kit thought he was going to live up to the Taggart reputation.

She waited with bated breath for the fireworks to begin. Instead, Boone inhaled deeply and settled back onto his heels with a shrug.

Bud draped the neatly coiled rope over his shoulder. "Your hoss," he said, sounding cocky and sure of himself now. He turned to his sister. "Ready to go, Sissy? Sissy!"

Sissy appeared to be in a sort of trance, staring at Boone as if he were a cool drink of lemonade in the middle of a hot afternoon. She licked her lips. "Uhhh . . . just a minute. I want to go to the little girls' room."

"Well, hurry up, will ya?"

Bud walked back to the truck. Boone leaned against the corral gate and stared thoughtfully at the black horse snorting and plunging across the way. Kit didn't know what she should do, because she didn't know quite what had happened.

"Kit!" It was Sissy.

"Yes, what?"

"I said, will you show me the way?"

Kit frowned. "You know the—"

"Kit!"

"Oh, okay, sure."

Mystified, she led Sissy into the house. Once in the hallway, Sissy spun around to peek through a window. "Okay, tell me everything," she commanded. "He's not married, is he? I didn't think so. Big-shot lawyer, been livin' in New York City and England, right? Is he serious about anyone? Ohhh, he's even cuter than he was when he played Sheriff Jack in Showdown Days! I swear, I could just eat him up with a spoon!"

"Have you gone loco?" Kit demanded. "That's just Boone, not Kevin Costner or somebody. The bathroom's—"

"I know where the bathroom is." Sissy licked her lips. "How long's he stayin'? Is he gonna have a part in Showdown Days? Oh, wow, that'd be great! I'll be Rose and he can be Sheriff Jack. . . . Ohhh, ohhh, ohhh!"

Ohhh, ohhh, ohhh, Kit thought. *Hold your breath!*

ONE THING she had to hand Boone, he only talked when he felt like it. Undressing that night for bed, she realized she'd spent the better part of the day trying to get a few words with him—okay, a lot of words. Trying, and failing. He'd spent hours locked up in Thom T.'s study with the telephone. She'd heard enough to know he'd been in touch with his office, with the family oil interests, even the cowboys Thom T. employed part-time to handle chores at the Rocking T.

There was so much more she wanted to know. Like what in the world he planned to do with that Outlaw horse; what, if anything, he planned to say to Thom T. about all this; and the really big one—had he lost his nerve?

Surely not, and yet . . .

In this part of the country, nobody respected a man who'd back away from a showdown. But that's exactly what Boone had done. Bud had questioned Boone's courage and lived—without a scratch—to tell about it.

Tossing and turning in bed, Kit fumbled for answers—and found none. She simply didn't know this Boone, so she was unable to fathom how his mind worked. This was not the boy she'd adored. That boy had been quick to laughter, easy to talk to and filled with a romantic gallantry that had thrilled her to the core—even when directed at other, older, girls.

Who had taken away that boy and sent this cold hard stranger in his place? She squeezed her eyes shut and willed sleep to come.

Through the moonlit night, she heard the sound of restless hooves in the corrals. Something was bothering the animals. She sat up in bed and strained to hear. Probably some wild critter passing through, a coyote maybe or even a polecat.

She lay back down, pulling the sheet over her shoulders in response to the air-conditioning. Her long cotton gown bunched around her hips and she struggled to untangle it—aha! Again she heard movement below, and this time she jumped out of bed and hurried to the window.

The barns and corrals lay in shadow. She couldn't make out much with her eyes, but her ears told her the animals were definitely nervous about something.

She hesitated. She could rouse Boone.

No way! She didn't need him. She'd go take a look herself. Lifting her gown above her knees, she stole barefoot from her room and crept down the stairs, avoiding the third one from the top—the one that squeaked. The front door stood unlocked, as was Thom T.'s custom. She slipped through it and down the broad steps into the yard.

Muggy heat struck her but she ignored it, running silently across the open ground to the nearest corral. Five horses paced inside. At her sudden appearance, they snorted and flung their heads. Carefully she inched around that corral to the next....

And saw what was spooking the animals. Blinking hard, she looked again.

Outlaw stood in the middle of the last enclosure, snubbed tight to the post in the center. What on earth?

Just then Boone walked out of the yawning blackness of the barn, a saddle thrown over one shoulder and a blanket in his hand. And she knew.

Here all alone in the middle of the night, Boone intended to ride the Outlaw.

CHAPTER THREE

KIT PRESSED BACK into the shadows, her heart in her throat, and watched Boone saddle the Outlaw. He was talking to the horse; she heard the soft murmur of his voice but couldn't make out the words. Outlaw arched his neck to look inquiringly at the man but made no protest.

Don't fall for that, Kit wanted to warn him. Thom T. took that black devil at his word and look where it got him. But she kept quiet. If Boone realized he had an audience, he would not be pleased.

Boone walked back into the barn, returning in a couple of minutes with some sort of cloth in his hands. Outlaw shied away, but the man persisted and soon was rubbing the animal down lightly, all the while talking, talking....

Kit eased herself down until she could sit on the ground and lean her elbows on the bottom rail. Boone was so intent on the horse that she felt fairly safe in changing her position. Even so, she took extreme care to remain in the shadows. Her white gown would reflect moonlight like a mirror if she made any sudden moves.

And she didn't want to miss anything. Boone was going to climb up on that bronc and heaven only knew what would happen when he did.

In the meantime, there was something curiously intimate about watching him. He handled the horse with total confidence, but gently, too, moving his hands and the cloth over and around and under the animal. Kit shivered despite the humid nighttime heat.

"Ready, old fellow?"

At the brisk tone of his voice, both Kit and the Outlaw snapped to attention. In a flash, Boone yanked the tether free and sprang into the saddle.

For a frozen moment, horse and rider stood silhouetted against the moon. Then all hell broke loose.

The horse's first wild leap nearly unseated his rider. Kit gripped the corral rail so hard her fingernails bit into the wood. How long had it been since Boone had ridden a bucker? Ten years, she figured; he probably didn't ride much at all back East. If he could just stay on board long enough to find his rhythm . . .

And he did. She could see him regain his balance and settle more securely into the saddle; she sensed the instant he began to challenge for control. He took everything the Outlaw could throw at him, his lean body swaying with the horse's stiff-legged gyrations.

And he took it with delight. He threw back his head and let out a cowboy yell, and Kit saw the flash of his teeth in the moonlight.

By the time the vicious bucking began to taper off, Kit was clinging weakly to a corral post. She'd seen a lot of bucking broncos both inside and outside a rodeo arena; she'd seen a lot of successful rides and nearly as many where the horse won. But she'd never seen anything to equal this. And Boone had done it in the middle of the night without—he thought—a single onlooker.

This was the kind of ride that made a man's reputation. Boone had mounted the horse with perfect confidence in the outcome, as far as she could see.

So why hadn't he called Bud's bluff? *Why didn't he call my bluff?*

The Outlaw had just about had enough. He went into a halfhearted series of crow hops, and she sensed Boone was beginning to relax in anticipation of certain victory. Time to start thinking about making a quiet getaway, she supposed, loath to do so.

She longed to make her presence known, shower him with the praise and admiration such a performance deserved. But if he'd wanted an audience he could have had one. The wisest thing to do was . . .

She stood up carefully, using both hands to hold her nightgown above her knees. Reluctantly she turned toward the house—just as something warm and furry and alive brushed the back of her calves.

With a panicky shriek, Kit bolted up the side of the corral. Heart thundering in her breast, she clung to the top rail, shaking with fear.

A FLASH OF WHITE rocked to the top of the corral, illuminated brilliantly in the moonlight. The unexpectedness of it startled Boone and spooked the horse. Outlaw flung his big body aside and right out from under his rider.

Boone hit the dirt hard enough to knock the breath out of him. He lay there gasping, wondering what the hell had happened.

"Boone! I'm sorry. I'm so sorry! Oh, what have I done?"

Kit flew across the enclosure to kneel beside him, her white cotton gown billowing around her. He felt her hands, softer and smaller than he'd have thought, touch his cheek.

"Speak to me!" she cried. "Oh, please, speak to me!"

She seemed to get hold of herself then; her hands ran over him with practiced skill, checking for broken bones. He lay there motionless, knowing he shouldn't, knowing he should tell her he was all right. It was childish to take advantage of her guilt, but to his surprise, he found he wasn't above doing that very thing—and enjoying it enormously.

Until she got to his ribs, which unfortunately had always been ticklish. When she slid her hands beneath his arms, he tried to channel his laughter into a groan—and failed.

"Daniel Boone Taggart!" She braced her hands on his shoulders and leaned down to peer into his face. "Are you playin' possum?"

He lifted his hands to her waist, crushing folds of white cotton around her. "Not possum, darlin'," he drawled in accents long suppressed but never forgotten. "I'm playin' somethin' en-*tar*-ly different."

His arms slid fully around her and Kit gave a little gasp of protest. Before she could marshal her defenses he pulled her down across his muscled chest and kissed her.

Once upon a time she had dreamed of Boone's kiss, but never like this, on the ground in the middle of a corral with a wild-eyed horse for an audience. She should cut this short in no uncertain terms, and yet....

She was melting beneath this softly teasing assault on her dignity—not to mention her self-control. Without thinking, she flowed against him, slid her hands up to cup his face and kissed him back.

Everything was going along just fine until the Outlaw nuzzled the small of her back. Startled, she tried to arch away from the horse's thrusting nose, which only succeeded in pressing her more closely against the man.

Who took unfair advantage by tightening his hold.

Spurred on by indignation, Kit managed to break away long enough to scramble across his recumbent form.

"What's the matter with that crazy horse?" she cried. "Shoo! Get away from here, Outlaw!"

She flapped her arms. The Outlaw flung up his head as if surprised by her lack of enthusiasm for his participation. In actual fact, now that she'd regained her senses, she felt considerable gratitude for his timely intrusion. Where that kiss might have led, heaven only knew.

Muffled laughter brought her attention swinging back to Boone. "And as for you...!" She glowered at him, speechless.

He started to sit up, groaned and slumped back. Her heart leapt in alarm, and contrition filled her. After all, *she* had caused him to take that bad spill. She was at fault; how could she have forgotten?

Again she crouched over him, touching his temples lightly. "Don't move," she instructed. "You may have a concussion. Does anything else hurt—besides your head, I mean?"

"Yes," he admitted in a wavering voice.

"What? Where?"

"Here," he said, clasping her hand and pressing it firmly against the unyielding wall of his chest. "I think it's... broken."

Oh, no, what had she done to him? Her palm tingled where it rested against his shirtfront, and her fingers arched into the warm flesh above the vee opening. "You think you've broken some ribs?" she inquired breathlessly. "Oh, Boone, I am *so* sorry."

"Not... ribs."

How weak he sounded; he must have been in shock when he kissed her, she decided. Otherwise he wouldn't have had the strength. "If it's not your ribs, then what is it?" With her free hand she brushed his tumbled hair away from his forehead.

"My... heart," he murmured piteously. "Broken..."

Kit sat back on her heels. "That doesn't make any sense," she announced. "You can't break a heart like you'd break a bone."

"You can if you're sufficiently humiliated!" His voice surged back strong and sure. He grabbed her by the upper arms and pulled her on top of him again. "Ol' Outlaw made a blasted fool out of me, but he didn't do it without help!"

He rolled over, pulling her with him. Suddenly she found herself flipped flat on her back looking up into his laughing face. Laughing!

She banged her fists against his chest with all her might. "Darn you, Boone, I thought you were really hurt! You scared me!" But his laughter was catching, and she couldn't resist joining in. It felt wonderful, laughing with him.

Too wonderful. She scrambled to a sitting position and wiped damp eyes. "Okay, I guess you got even," she admitted grudgingly.

"You think so?" He also sat up, moving more gingerly. With one hand he carefully explored his left cheekbone. "I'm not so sure. What made you lose your head like that?"

"A cat." She wondered if she sounded as sheepish as she felt. "I was getting ready to go back into the house...."

"How long'd you been there?"

"Uhhh... the whole time. But I wasn't spying, honest. I heard the horses making a commotion and came out to see what was bothering them."

"Right." He looked her over with exaggerated care. "In your nightgown in the dark. Were you expecting rustlers, or simply a band of marauding bobcats?"

She felt her cheeks flame. "I wasn't expecting anything, to tell you the truth. If I'd found something I
wouldn't have done anything stupid. I...I'd probably just
have gone to get you."

"Probably." Again the white flash of his smile. "What
do you do when I'm not here and Thom T.'s laid up with
a broken leg? Who do you get then?"

She shifted uncomfortably. "Up to this point, the
question's never arisen."

"But if it does?" he persisted.

"I guess I'd get the shotgun off the gun rack in Thom
T.'s study."

Boone groaned. "And shoot yourself, I don't doubt."

But he didn't go on to stress the obvious—that she really wasn't able to take up all the slack left by Thom T.'s
injury. She was grateful he didn't push her into that argument right on the spot.

Because she didn't feel like arguing. Sitting there on the
hard-packed earth with him, moonlight streaming around
them, the last thing she felt like doing was defending her
position. This was one of the goofiest things that had ever
happened to her, but in other ways, among the most
pleasant. Suddenly self-conscious, she glanced down at
her nightgown, then at him. She caught her breath in
surprise.

"Why, you're wearing jeans!" she exclaimed. "And
boots. And a plain old workshirt! Will wonders never
cease?"

"What can I say?" He shrugged and spread his hands
wide. "When in Rome—or in this case, when in Texas..."
He stood, then leaned down to offer her a hand up.

After the briefest of hesitations, she accepted his assistance. He wasn't only dressed differently, he was also
speaking differently—or the same, depending on your

perspective. Texas was back in his voice. He was seeming more and more like the old Boone, the one she'd been crazy about—in her youth, of course. But there was still one thing she didn't understand.

"Why did you wait until no one was around to ride the Outlaw?" she blurted. "After what Bud said . . ."

"Ah." He still held her hand in his, but lightly. His face was in shadow, his voice serious. "I had nothing to prove, Kitty—certainly not to Bud Williams."

"But what about—" She bit off the final word *me!*

"Why, Kitty McCrae!" The drawl was thick as honey now. "Don't tell me yawl thought poorly of me!"

"I wouldn't have, if you'd been like this."

"Like what?"

"Like—" she shrugged helplessly "—like the Boone I knew before you went away. I . . . I don't much care for the new you, if you want to know the truth."

"Oh, I want the truth all right."

She narrowed her eyes, trying to see his expression clearly enough to determine the degree of his sincerity. "Big-shot international lawyers aren't my cup of tea," she said airily. She pulled her hand from his, not needing that distraction.

"But that's who I am now." The seriousness had returned. "And I worked damned hard to get there."

"Maybe so, but you know what Thom T. always says—'You can take the boy out of the country—'"

"—'but you can't take the country outta the boy.' Yeah, I know. In this case, he's wrong. This—" he indicated his clothing "—is nothing more than a walk down memory lane. I found this stuff in the back of my closet and couldn't resist."

"I think it's the real you," she said stubbornly.

He gave a bark of laughter. "I'm not John Wayne, Kitty. Hell, I'm not even Kevin Costner. I'm a big-time Yankee lawyer who eats little girls like you for breakfast." He took a step toward her.

She took a corresponding step back. "I don't believe you!" She didn't *want* to believe him, anyway.

"Suit yourself. Just don't get your hopes up that at the last minute I'll see things your way, because it ain't gonna happen."

His words sent a cold chill down her spine. It would be very easy to get her hopes up where he was concerned— about a lot of things.

"Time will tell," she said tartly. "Once again, my apologies. Even Jesse couldn't have given the Outlaw a better ride."

"Even Jesse, huh? I'm flattered."

"You should be." She lifted her chin defiantly.

"Well, I am, because any way you cut it, the horse won this round. Of course, it took a little help from the peanut gallery."

With a last mortified glance in his direction, she picked up the hem of her gown and hurried through the moonlight. His soft laughter followed.

And that night it haunted her dreams.

RITA DROPPED BY the next day—Thursday—to pick up a folder she'd forgotten on her previous visit. Drinking lemonade with Kit on the glass-enclosed porch, she sighed and leaned back in her wicker chair.

"Showdown Days will be the death of me," she predicted. "Harry Meeks is trying to chicken out, and if he does, we're all up the creek without a paddle."

Kit, who had been watching Boone cross the ranch yard, tried to pull her attention back to the business at hand. He looked so sleek and civilized today that she wondered if she'd been hallucinating last night. He disappeared around a corner of the house, and she turned toward her companion. "Which part is Harry's?"

"Boone, the Mysterious Gunfighter. Although Bud Williams would be much better—he did that part last year and he's got the gunfighter mentality, that's for sure."

"Which is?"

Rita raised one eyebrow. "An inclination to go through something without even looking for a way around it."

She seemed so pleased with herself that Kit laughed. "That's Bud all right. But then who would play noble Sheriff Jack?"

"Who indeed." Rita sighed. "Boone would be great—your Boone, I mean. Think we can talk him into it?"

"He's not 'my' Boone, and what's this 'we' stuff?"

"We—you, me, Thom T., the entire cast, the mayor, the population of Showdown."

Kit shook her head. "No way. In the first place, he's not going to be here that long. In the second place, he wants no truck with that sort of thing. He's changed, Rita, major big time."

Rita looked doubtful. "He may have changed but he's still a Taggart. It's *his* great-great-aunt or whatever who started all this, for pity's sake."

"He wouldn't even consider it. Trust me."

"But he did it before, and very well, I might add." Rita smiled confidently. "And he'd be better now. Then he was a charming boy. Now he's...all...grown...up."

She sounded so suggestive that Kit had to swallow hard before she could answer. "Go for it if it'll make you happy. I think you're wasting your time, but if you want to ask him—"

The inner door opened and Boone walked out onto the porch. "Ask who what?" he inquired, adding a belated, "Hi, Rita. How are you?"

Rita straightened in her chair and deposited her empty glass on a small table. "Depends. How long you gonna be in town, Boone?"

He raised his brows in polite surprise. "Depends. Not long, though."

"Four weeks—that's my interpretation of 'depends, not long.'" She exchanged a pointed glance with Kit, who rolled her eyes. "How'd you like to play Sheriff Jack, the Hero of Showdown Days?"

"Not even a little—"

"No, don't thank me." Rita gave him a brilliant smile and waved his objections aside—or tried to. "Just come to the committee meeting and I'll introduce you as—"

"Rita!"

She blinked. "Yes?"

"Thanks but no thanks. I've sort of grown past the age and stage where I enjoy dressing up and playing cowboy."

Rita's eyes widened and Kit saw genuine alarm there. "If that's the truth, I feel sorry for you, Daniel Boone Taggart. Next you're going to tell me you don't believe in fairies."

"Bite your tongue." Boone's mouth twitched in that almost grin, and his eyes sparkled. "I'm from New York City! However, I do have my doubts about our local legend."

"Swell," Kit put in. "You had your moment of stardom as Noble Sheriff Jack and now you want to rain on our parade."

He crossed to the lemonade pitcher and looked around for a clean glass. Seeing none, he picked up Kit's empty one, refilled it and drank deep. "Nope," he said, his tongue flicking out at the corner of his mouth. "But as the whole world knows, it's *my* many-times-great-aunt whose adventures are chronicled every year. That does give me a proprietary interest."

He set down the glass and walked to the door. "Poor Rose. I'll bet she was nowhere close to the simpering goody two-shoes paraded out for Showdown Days." He gave them a whimsical look. "Too bad there's no way to know for sure. We could change history."

The two women watched him go, then traded glances. Kit gave an "I told you so" shrug.

Rita sighed. "Lord, he'd be *wonderful,*" she said in a voice full of longing. "There must be a way to talk him into it...."

IF THERE WAS, Kit had no time to worry about it. Thom T. was on the prod. When Doc Preston dropped by late in the afternoon, the old man asked Kit to fetch a pitcher of iced tea and then make herself scarce. The doctor shrugged and settled himself into a chair, the soul of patience, although he and Kit both knew his wife wasn't going to like his coming home late for dinner.

Boone started to pull up a chair for himself but Thom T. stopped him. "You, too, boy. What goes on between a man and his doctor is private."

"But—"

Dr. Preston raised his hands in a conciliatory gesture. "We'll talk before I leave," he promised.

So Kit and Boone ended up waiting together on the porch, he sitting nonchalantly in a wicker chair while she paced.

And all the while she watched him surreptitiously, admiring his easy manner but not his iron control. After a while she paused and said, "I noticed the Outlaw isn't in the corral anymore. What did you do with him?"

"Moved him to the north pasture. More privacy there." His mouth curved up at one corner.

Kit jammed her hands into her jeans pockets and rocked back on her heels, curiosity getting the better of her. "Did you tell Thom T. what happened?"

A broad grin broke through. "Sure. He loved it. Made his own run-in with old Outlaw a little easier to take, knowing his grandson's luck wasn't a helluva lot better."

She smiled back at him, thinking he was even more attractive when he let himself relax. "In all fairness, you were doing fine until I ruined things."

"I didn't even mention you were there."

"Why on earth not? I'm ready to accept the blame."

"What's the point? It might worry him, knowing you run around outdoors in the middle of the night. At the very least he'd think I was trying to hide behind a woman's skirts—or in this case, nightgown. Thanks but no thanks."

Kit drew an exasperated breath. "But he's sure to mention it to someone sooner or later, and everybody in town will know the Outlaw claimed another victim," she argued. "It's not fair to *you*, Boone."

"I'm not going to be around long enough for it to matter."

She caught her breath at his matter-of-fact announcement. She'd said practically the same thing to Rita, but hearing him verify her prediction still came as something of a shock. All she could say was a weak, "Oh!"

All the good humor was gone from his expression. "I do have a job, responsibilities. The longer I'm gone, the harder it will be to—" He broke off to stare moodily through the glass louvers at the sun-washed Texas landscape. After a moment, he said, "How long do you think it will be before Thom T.'s up and around?"

"W-why..." She pressed her lips together, wondering how much she should say. "It depends," she hedged.

"But not long."

"Probably not."

"Good. Because as soon as he's in shape to travel, I plan to take him back East with me—"

"No!" She pressed one hand to her chest.

"For a *visit*. The change of scene will do him good and give me a chance to clear up a few pressing matters at my office. Might even convince him that New York is more than just a city. But when I take him out of here, he has to go willingly."

"Oh, Boone, no." Miserably she stared down at the pointed toes of her boots. "I thought... I hoped...."

"That I'd reconsidered? Just because I haven't been talking about unloading this place doesn't mean that anything's changed."

"Unload!" Offended, she whirled away, hands tightening into fists. "How can you be so insensitive? The history of the Taggart family was written here—the history of the entire town, for that matter. It makes me furious to hear you—"

"Ahem." Dr. Preston paused in the doorway, clearing his throat noisily. He glanced from Kit to Boone and back again, his glance bright and interested. "You had some questions?" he reminded Boone.

"Right." Boone escorted the doctor toward the outer door. "I just wanted to get some idea when the old scalawag's going to be up and around again, Doctor. Kit's already told me that..."

The two men left the porch and walked toward the doctor's big black Lincoln. Kit stared after them, feeling betrayed. Boone had already messed up her world, but it was nothing compared to what he was prepared to do.

What was she prepared to do to stop him?

SHE WAS STILL WRESTLING with that question at five-thirty when she opened the door to admit Jenny Merton. Jenny, a licensed vocational nurse who worked for Dr. Preston, was the only other medical practitioner Kit knew who was willing to brave Thom T.'s mercurial temperament. In fact, the middle-aged and motherly Jenny actually seemed to enjoy matching words and wits with her irascible patient.

"Yawl take your time and have fun, honey," she told Kit. "After being cooped up for a week with that man you deserve it!"

"Thanks, but I won't be long." Kit slung her bag over her shoulder. "The Showdown Days Committee meeting is at six and I'll be home soon as it's over."

"Don't rush back on my account." Jenny craned her neck to look around. "I hear Boone's back," she said, her eyes bright and inquisitive. "Also hear that big black Outlaw hoss throwed him but good!"

Great, Kit thought. Score another point for the local grapevine. "I guess so."

"Sure would'a liked to see that." Jenny walked over to peer down the hallway. "Well, where is he? Sissy tells me he's cuter'n a little speckled pup."

Kit laughed. "I don't know where he is at the moment. He drove away almost an hour ago."

Jenny sighed heavily but her eyes twinkled. "Oh, well, I can live with disappointment."

Thom T.'s bell tinkled loudly, followed by his bellow: "Kit, you still there, or you gone off and left me at th' mercy a' Joe Starky's middle gal? Gol dang it, somebody answer me!''

Automatically Kit started for the hall, but Jenny caught her arm. "Let me handle this, honey," she advised, giving a hitch to the jeans she wore beneath her pale pink uniform smock. "I'm just in the mood to tangle with that old buzzard. Might even whup him in a game of checkers."

SO WHO SHOULD BE STANDING outside the room where the Showdown Days Committee was scheduled to meet? Boone, naturally. Kit glared at him. "What in the world are *you* doing here?" she demanded.

He took her arm and turned her toward the door. "I decided to drop by to protect my family honor," he said.

She couldn't tell if he was serious or teasing; whichever the case, he had every right to be here if he chose. But his presence certainly didn't do much for her equilibrium.

He opened the door and she walked in ahead of him. Approximately two dozen people were already there, and every single one of them turned to look at Kit and Boone. And keep on looking.

"What?" she demanded irritably of everyone in general. "I'm not late, am I?"

Heads shook solemnly.

"Did I forget to put on all my clothes?" She pretended to take inventory. "Nope, got my jeans, got my shirt, got my boots."

The smiles grew wider. "This *is* the meeting of the Showdown Days Committee, right?" She put her hands on her hips and cocked her head to one side.

"Right—that's right," several voices responded.

Kit indicated herself. "And I *am* Kit McCrae, assistant chairman for the upcoming fiesta."

"Aha!" Rita stepped forward, her smile the widest of all. "That's where you're wrong. Who you are is Rose Taggart, heroine extraordinaire! Congratulations, Kit. You are the selection committee's unanimous choice!"

Kit's mouth fell open in shock as the wave of applause swept over her.

CHAPTER FOUR

ROSE TAGGART! To Kit, Rose was Miss America and the Queen of England rolled up together. Like virtually every other unmarried woman in Showdown, she'd secretly dreamed of some day being chosen to star in her own version of the local legend, but she'd never expected the dream to come true.

Accepting the hugs and congratulations of the other committee members, she blinked back happy tears. That something so wonderful could happen to Kit McCrae, thirteen years after being dumped on the doorstep at the Rocking T like so much dirty laundry, seemed a miracle.

Being chosen to play Rose meant she was accepted here in her adopted hometown. It meant that for once in her life she belonged.

Eyes misty, she felt a hand on her elbow and turned inquiringly to find Boone standing there. She braced herself for his scorn, knowing he thought the whole thing silly—much ado about nothing. *Please, not now,* she begged silently. *Later you can say anything you want, but please don't spoil my moment.*

Reluctantly she met his gaze. He smiled and her heart skipped a beat, then raced double time.

"Congratulations," he said in a husky voice. "You playing Rose makes us kissing cousins—sort of."

He bent his head and she waited in breathless anticipation, her throat tight and dry. At the last instant he
corrected his aim to drop a light kiss on her nose.

"Okay, okay, people, if you'll all take your seats we
have other business to attend to."

It was Rita, getting the meeting back on track. Numbly
Kit sank onto the nearest folding metal chair, Boone settling beside her. Taking a deep breath, she tried to calm
herself.

Rita consulted a clipboard. "The first order of business, as I'm sure you're all aware, is to set an accelerated
rehearsal schedule." She pursed her lips and looked up
sharply, her intent gaze zeroing in on Boone.

"Boone Taggart," she announced, "I'm giving you one
more chance. What would it take to get you to play the
part of Jack, the Noble Sheriff?"

"It would take," Boone said in steely tones, "an act of
God. Rita, I've already told you that I don't consider this
annual orgy of myth and legend to be so much historical
as hysterical. I've got no problem with it, understand—I
don't know of anyone it hurts, and it's good for local
business. But neither do I have any interest in perpetuat-
ing what, in all frankness, seems like little more than another tall Texas tale."

"Boone Taggart, bite your tongue!" Sissy Williams
stared at him, wide-eyed. "Yawl don't have a whole lotta
respect for your ancestors, I'd say."

Boone shrugged. "That's not how I see it."

"Hold on, hold on." Rita held up her hands in a gesture meant to calm. "Boone, when Showdown Days first
started about fifty years ago, a lot of effort went into historical research. We may fudge a teeny bit here and there
in the interests of drama, but I'm satisfied the story is es-
sentially correct."

"Good for you," Boone responded promptly.

"But you're not satisfied, I take it."

He raised his brows and shrugged again.

"Then bring me proof and we'll change the script."

"Hey, it's not that important to me. Do whatever you want. Just include me out."

Rita glared at him. "I'm serious. Your family honor's at stake. If you can provide proof—old letters, diaries, whatever—we'll certainly accommodate you. Do you have such proof?"

"I've never cared enough to look for it," Boone admitted without the slightest trace of remorse. "We've got an attic full of family stuff—but we digress. You asked if I wanted to play Sheriff Jack and I said thanks but no thanks."

He leaned back in the chair and crossed his arms. His expression, Kit thought, betrayed a hint of smugness.

"Okay, I got it." Rita regarded him through narrowed eyes. "The Noble Sheriff is out." She brightened. "So how'd you like to play the Mysterious Gunslinger?"

A wave a laughter ranging from nervous to incredulous swept the room. Boone groaned. "*If* I were going to get involved in this goofy undertaking, *if* I were willing to make a public spectacle of myself, *if* I could find any reason on God's green earth to get involved in Showdown Days, *then* I'd vastly prefer the part of the Mysterious Gunslinger to that of the goody-goody sheriff."

"So, does that mean . . . ?" Rita took an eager step forward, clutching her clipboard to her chest.

"It *means* thanks but no thanks." His expression left no room whatsoever for negotiation.

"Well, I tried," Rita announced crisply. "Henceforth kindly keep your doubts to yourself unless you come bearing proof."

She dismissed him with a toss of her head. "Here we go, folks. Principles—Bud Williams as Sheriff Jack, Harry Meeks as the Mysterious Gunfighter, Lee Cox as Rose's Protective Brother James, and Rose of course—your schedule will be as follows..."

Rita began listing dates and times, but Kit found it difficult to pay proper attention. She was still too excited about being chosen, but that was only part of it. The rest was Boone.

He hadn't seemed the least bit offended by Rita's determination to get him involved. At the moment, he listened to the plan unfold with obvious interest, the shadow of a smile curving his lips.

Still, she reminded herself, he had passed up a chance to play hero to her heroine. What might that have been like? She shivered and tried to concentrate on Rita's instructions.

BOONE DROVE into San Antonio early the next morning for unspecified purposes. That left Kit to share the midday meal alone with Thom T., a prospect that pleased her. The old man was cross and complaining about his cast, so she didn't bring up Showdown Days until they were on their tapioca pudding.

He listened closely while she told him that she had been chosen to play Rose. "And then Rita tried to get Boone to take a part, but he wouldn't even consider it." Her tone was condemning. "He seemed to have a few doubts about the legend's veracity."

Thom T. snorted. "Pure hogwash," he pronounced.

Kit frowned. "Boone's attitude?"

"Nope. That show they put on ever' year."

Kit slumped, feeling deflated as a flat tire. "What are you saying?" she wailed. "I've never heard you suggest anything like this before. If they're—if we're not doing it right, why didn't you speak up sooner?''

"Because," he said, leaning back against his pillows, "I didn't know it at first. Suspected, mind you, but didn't know."

"And now you do?"

He squinted at her thoughtfully. "This botherin' you, gal? You takin' it personal?"

Kit managed a pained smile. "No. Yes. It's just that...it'd be my luck to have the greatest honor of my life blow up in my face before I can enjoy it."

He patted her hand and smiled. "Well, I won't be the one that does it. Way I figger, even if it ain't gospel truth, where's the harm?"

She supposed. "Still, now my curiosity's up. Would you mind if I took a look later at that old stuff up in the attic?"

After the briefest of hesitations, he nodded. "Help yourself. Just don't blame me if you find out things you'd sooner not know."

"I promise I won't." She rose and picked up the lunch tray. "There's a couple more servings of tapioca pudding if you'd like seconds."

Thom T. licked his lips. "Much obliged. Another dish of that fish-eye puddin' is just what I need."

So she brought him another dessert, and then she helped him up to sit in a chair for a while, and then she tucked him back into bed and read to him from one of his favorite Louis L'Amour books.

Hours later, she made her way up the stairs. As she eased open the door to the attic, she caught her breath.

Sunlight streamed through gabled windows at each end, illuminating the cluttered room in dancing motes of dust. It seemed as if every inch of space was packed and piled high with boxes, old furniture, and odds and ends of every description.

For a moment Kit simply stood there, stunned by the bounty before her. This was history—very personal family history. A tide of envy, hot and suffocating, rose in her chest. She closed her eyes and drew a deep shaky breath.

So many Taggarts had contributed to this treasure trove of memorabilia. Generations of Taggarts followed each behind the other in an unbroken line that stretched back to the birth of Texas—even farther.

Stepping up to an old walnut buffet stacked with cartons, Kit opened the nearest one and peered inside. The first item she found was a scrap of needlepoint, not quite finished.

With her fingertips she touched the faded yarn letters: "Remember Me." A tiny rose embellished one corner.

A curious premonition settled over her, causing the hair on the nape of her neck to prickle. She would swear that this was Rose Taggart's work. She felt a sort of psychic energy in her fingertips, and her heart beat faster.

Quickly putting down the needlework, she reached for the next item, a lace handkerchief yellow with age. She examined it, noticing the initials "D.L." in one corner. Could this have belonged to Thom T.'s grandmother Diana? What had been her maiden name?

Too much. Too much to see and touch and explore. Kit looked around helplessly. She felt a sense of awe just being here. More than anything, she wished that these were *her* memories of *her* family.

But her own memories, at least the early ones, were entirely different. . . .

Kit's mother had always told her she was born in Hollywood. She was ten or eleven when she finally took a look at her birth certificate and realized she'd been born in Salinas.

She'd confronted her mother about this discrepancy. Eileen had smiled and patted her daughter's cheek. "But wouldn't you rather be born in Hollywood?" she'd asked in that gently reproachful tone she always took with Kit.

That wasn't the only jolt Kit got from her birth certificate. She'd thought her father's name was Jock Mc-Crae; that was what Mother had always said, although he'd disappeared before Kit was even born. To her shock and horror, she saw a name listed that she'd never even heard of.

But she'd never mentioned that to Mother, choosing instead to zero in on the Hollywood-Salinas discrepancy. She was much, much older before she realized that "John Doe" probably wasn't her father's name, either. By then Eileen was dead and Kit was attending college and had other worries.

Kit grew up in Southern California, surrounded by palm trees, sunshine and, more often than not, strangers. Eileen was an actress looking for her big break. While she looked, she worked at whatever jobs she could find—cosmetic salesclerk was a favorite, because she was so pretty.

The young Kit was an independent little thing; that was what Mother and Aunt June said, and that was what she remembered. Early on she discovered that her red hair was practically a license to be eccentric. "Her temper sure matches her hair" was a remark she heard often.

To those who showed her kindness, Kit gave her heart. Her mother was always kind, even though she sometimes went on location for films and left Kit with the landlady. When Eileen returned she always brought her daughter some small present, but that wasn't what mattered to Kit. What mattered was the return of her anchor.

Then when she was twelve, the good-natured landlady sold the apartment building and moved away. Kit felt cast adrift; all she had left was a mother who flitted in and out like a butterfly. Then she lost that foundation, too.

Not to death—Eileen lived another seven years. No, she lost out to time and circumstances beyond her control. Kit was getting too old; she looked too mature, Eileen said, and there was no longer a safe place to stash her while Eileen worked.

Patiently, with a practiced little catch in her voice, Eileen explained that she wasn't getting the roles she should, because, with a nearly grown daughter in the wings ... She knew Kit wouldn't want to stand in the way of her mother's happiness and success.

Wouldn't Kit like to visit Aunt June in Texas for a while? Just think! A ranch with cowboys and horses!

Don't worry, Eileen said; it's only temporary. She was up for a big part in a high-class production, and as soon as she nailed it, she'd come get Kit and they'd be together again, just like always.

Kit, her heart breaking, pretended to believe. It wasn't pride that made her lie; it was the knowledge that the decision had already been made—and fear that if she created a fuss, she'd never see her mother again.

If she was a very, very good girl, if she did everything she was told without complaint, helped Aunt June and didn't cause anybody any problems, maybe, just maybe...

So she decided to blend into the woodwork; nobody would even know she was there. She wasn't going to get close to anybody and nobody was going to get close to her while she waited for her mother to retrieve her.

That's how she planned it, but that's not how it happened.

Standing in the hot stillness of the Taggart attic, Kit lived again the day she came to the Rocking T for the first time. Aunt June had picked up the twelve-year-old at the bus station in San Antonio. Aunt June was nice—much older than her sister Eileen, and not nearly so pretty, but motherly and smiling and apparently happy to see her niece.

Aunt June had been married a long time ago, and she'd had one son who died, Kit's mother had told her. She'd been housekeeper at the ranch in Texas for at least ten years.

After what seemed to Kit like an endless drive, they pulled into the ranch yard at the Rocking T, stopping in front of a house bigger and nicer than any she'd ever been inside. Without waiting to be told, she got out of the car with her one suitcase and her shopping bag of treasures. Then she just stood there, wondering what was going to happen next, wondering what Mother had got her into this time. Scared—yes, she was scared.

Aunt June grinned. "Yore home, honey!" she announced.

And down the steps of that beautiful white house came this ramrod straight man with silver hair, and two boys a few years older than Kit. They were all smiling in welcome. They scared her so bad she'd have turned around and run if Aunt June hadn't hung on to her shoulder.

"Howdy, little lady," said the silver-haired man, stopping in front of Kit. He flung his arms wide to hold back the two boys threatening to run her over in their enthusiasm. "Welcome to the Rocking T."

It must have been the way he'd said "welcome," as if
he really meant it. She couldn't think why else she would
have burst into tears.

That was her introduction to Thom T. It seemed as if
she'd begun to love him that very first day, although it was
much later before she admitted it. Sternly he ordered the
older boy—Jesse, Kit soon learned, who was nineteen;
Boone was seventeen—to take her suitcase to "her"
room. That surprised her, although where else they might
have put her she hadn't stopped to consider—a closet
somewhere, maybe.

While she was still standing there awkwardly puzzling
it out, Boone reached for her shopping bag. That bag
contained her most treasured possessions: a few books, an
autographed picture of Harrison Ford in his *Star Wars*
costume obtained especially for her by her mother, a ticket
stub from a Hollywood premiere of some quickly forgotten picture—precious memories all.

She yanked the bag away and glared at Boone through
her tears. He pulled back, his eyes wide and surprised. She
saw at once she'd made a mistake; he'd only been trying
to help. There was nothing in that bag he'd want, and now
she'd offended him.

She started to stammer an apology, but he winked and
shoved his hands deep into his jeans pockets. Embarrassed, she stood there with her head hanging. Then she
heard Boone say gently, "We've got a new litter of kit-
tens in the barn. Want to see 'em?"

That was when she'd started loving Boone.

So long ago...

Kit picked up a volume bound in faded red leather and
let its pages fall open in her hands. The handwriting was
dim and difficult to decipher. She flipped through a few
pages, looking for a name, a date, anything to indicate

authorship. Finding none, she laid the diary down and considered her next move.

A steamer trunk, wedged behind a tower of boxes next to one dust-streaked window, caught her restless glance. With a little cry of pleasure, she worked her way toward it. Perhaps Thom T. wouldn't mind if she dragged the trunk downstairs and cleaned it up. It was far too wonderful to be shunted aside in a dusty old attic.

Reaching the trunk, she cleared out a space around it, moving boxes and rearranging an old pair of lamps and several wicker baskets. It was hot up here; she felt a tickle of perspiration on her temple and wiped it away with her shirttail.

The trunk was locked, but someone had hung a ring of keys conveniently on a nail beside the window. A few moments of trial and error and the lid to the trunk swung open.

Tissue paper, dark and stiff with age, obscured the contents. When Kit touched the paper, it crumbled into dust. Reaching inside, she carefully drew out . . .

A wedding dress! She caught her breath and stared at the glorious confection of satin and lace. Handling the gown as if it, too, might disintegrate, she turned slowly around until she could see herself reflected in the cloudy mirror of an old dresser against the opposite wall.

Was this Diana's dress, or maybe even Rose's? Which Taggart bride had walked down the aisle to meet the man she loved wearing this wonderful, wonderful gown? Kit pressed her cheek against the antique satin, tears pricking behind her eyelids. To meet the man she loved . . .

At twelve she'd loved Boone Taggart. And because she loved him, she feared it would be only a matter of time before he, too, would leave her as her mother had. And soon after she came to the Rocking T, he did—he went off to college. After that she lived for his vacations, and for that part of each summer when he'd come home.

But the older he got, the less time he had for her, although he was never deliberately unkind. When he was with her, she got all his attention—and loved it. Whether horseback riding or swimming in the creek, clearing the dishes from the table or mucking out stalls, Boone could make anything seem like an incredible adventure.

To her dazzled eyes at fourteen, he was the most handsome, brave, *heroic* man in the world. For the first time she'd allowed herself to believe that someone could be a permanent fixture in her life.

Boone was her knight in shining armor. Some day he'd sweep in on a white horse and carry her away, just like in the fairy tales. She could count on Boone, she told herself. Always.

What she would later call her childish infatuation peaked the summer she was fifteen and he was twenty-one, between college and law school—or as Thom T. said, "between hay and grass." That was the summer he played Sheriff Jack in the Showdown Days celebration.

That event must have represented a sort of last fling for him, Kit realized later. He was gearing up for Harvard Law School. There'd be no time or energy left for anything else once he went East in the fall. It was as if he'd decided to usher out his boyhood with a bang.

Adoring him, she watched his shenanigans with her heart on her sleeve. She was no longer twelve years old; at almost-sixteen she thought she was a woman. She'd been kissed—all right, only once and she didn't much like it—but she was confident she knew all about the birds and the bees. She even got a part in Showdown Days herself—just a face in the crowd, but at least she had a front-row seat . . . to watch *him*.

She didn't like what she saw. Boone flirted outrageously with Marcella What's-Her-Face, that year's Rose; he came home late with lipstick on his collar. Enraged, Kit stopped speaking to him; she got even angrier when he didn't seem to notice.

Then it was all over and time for him to leave for Harvard.

Standing before the mirror now, holding a beautiful old wedding gown up in front of her, Kit remembered the day he left, remembered the unhappy girl sitting on the glider in the shade of a clump of cottonwood trees trying not to cry. Something wonderful had ended and she knew it even then.

Boone had come out of the house and walked over to her. Kneeling, he picked up her hands, which were clenched together on her knee. His face was sad and serious.

"Byo, Kitty Cat," he said softly. "Don't forget me, you hear?" He lifted her hands and kissed them, his beautiful blue-gray eyes kind.

She couldn't let him leave like that—her breaking heart wouldn't permit it. She took hold of her courage, pulled her hands free and planted one on each side of his face. "Boone," she whispered, "I love you." She held her breath.

He smiled. "I love you, too," he said very gently. "You be a good girl, now. Any a' them no-account Showdown boys mess with you, tell 'em they'll have to answer to Daniel Boone Taggart."

He'd winked, leaned forward and dropped a kiss on her nose—the same kind of kiss he'd given her the other night when she was named this year's Rose. Then he'd got up and walked away, and that was that.

Staring at her reflection in the smoky mirror, Kit clamped her lips tightly together. He'd been tacky old Marcella's hero, playing Sheriff Jack with more verve than anyone before or since. Now it was Kit's turn to be the heroine and who was her hero? Bud Williams, a good ol' boy who'd been trying to trap her in the back seat of a car ever since she'd come home to Showdown.

Carefully she laid aside the gown and began stripping off her clothes. She could still remember the dashing way Boone performed his role, the way he swept Marcella into his arms while proclaiming, "Rose, my beloved, you will be mine!"

Marcella not only would, Kit always suspected she *had*. Drat! She kicked off her boots and shoved her jeans down, stepping out to flick them aside with one foot. She probably wouldn't even be able to get the gown closed around her, but she was going to try!

Yanking the T-shirt over her head, she dropped it and picked up the wedding dress, her touch reverent. It took some time to separate all the layers, find the proper route to poke her head through, maneuver her arms into the sleeves. She worked very carefully, almost holding her breath. The garment was old—more than a hundred years, probably—and fragile. Although she felt confident Thom T. wouldn't object to what she was doing, she'd cut off her arm before she'd damage so much as a single stitch.

At last her head poked through the mountain of lace and fabric. With painstaking care, she gently worked the yards of material down and settled the skirt over her hips. Straightening, she stretched to fumble at the tiny pearl buttons and loop closures in back.

It was slow and tedious work. Starting from the bottom of the placket closing, she worked her way to the waist, took a deep breath and sucked in as much as she possibly could.

Oh, Lord, the edges barely met. Five pounds, that was all it'd take and she'd be able to wear the gown. Holding the waist closed with one hand, she turned right and left, peering at herself in the mirror. Her curly red hair fell across her eyes, and impatiently she used her free hand to sweep the unruly locks to the top of her head.

There, that looked better. Finally getting a good view, she began to smile. It was a wonderful dress, wonderful! She'd never worn anything so exquisite. She felt like a princess, a queen . . . a bride. If she put her hair up so . . .

Turning away from the mirror, she twisted to look back over her shoulder to get the full glorious effect of the graceful train. For the first time in her life, she felt truly beautiful. Standing there in the hot musty attic, she smiled a slow secret smile . . . just as her gaze met Boone's in the mirror.

CHAPTER FIVE

BOONE HAD COME to the attic in search of a cane for Thom T., but now he stood mesmerized, watching Kit pirouette slowly and gracefully in the overheated attic. Her momentum carried her around and their glances locked in the mirror. She stopped short, the glorious flounces and ruffles of the wedding gown swirling around her to settle in a frothy cloud.

The gown was no match for the woman....

Light beams sliced through the dusky room, highlighting the magnificent red hair piled atop her head. Dust particles danced around her like fairy beams, heightening the sense of unreality.

This wasn't little Kitty McCrae standing before him; this was a beautiful desirable woman.

KIT CAUGHT HER BREATH at the expression on his face. Her hand—the one holding her hair up—dropped to press against her throat. The fiery mane tumbled around her shoulders but she barely noticed. Had her unruly thoughts conjured up the very Taggart for whom she longed?

He took one step, and froze. For a moment they stood there staring at each other. Then, as if in the grip of some powerful unseen force, they moved together. Kit felt as if she were floating, so intense was the sense of unreality. Their gazes still locked, they stopped of mutual accord, just short of touching.

He said her name like a question, as if he had trouble believing it was indeed she. The sound of his voice broke through some final fragile barrier. With a sigh, she melted into his opening arms.

They kissed . . . kissed again. His hand brushed across the open back of her gown; when he touched bare skin she felt his shocked reaction. Taking instant advantage, he curved his hand around her ribs, inside the satin bodice.

She arched closer to him, lost in a haze of longing. His lips were at once tender and demanding, his touch coaxing and clever. Her inhibitions took flight along with her heart; she felt his hands on her shoulders, gently easing down the bodice of the gown. Resistance was the last thing in her mind—

"*Kit! Boone!* If one a' you don't fetch that gol-durned cane I'm gettin' outta this bed if I hav'ta fly!"

Thom T.'s familiar and querulous tone effectively shattered the enchantment. Kit stiffened; Boone uttered a ragged groan and stood her away from him, at the same time smoothing the gown back over her shoulders. She stared at him, shocked at what had happened—more shocked at what *could* have happened.

He stared back, his eyes dark and filled with passion. "If you're expecting an apology, you can forget it." His gaze scanned her features, ending on lips swollen and tender from his kisses. "The fact is, I enjoyed kissing you the other night in the corral. I liked it even more just now."

"*What in hades you two doin' up there? If one a' you don't get in here I'm gonna dial 911, I swear it!*"

Kit reached around to tug at the open edges of the gown. "You're embarrassing me." The admission almost choked her.

"I know." He gave her the old lopsided grin she remembered. "You're blushing."

She squeezed her eyes closed in mortification. "Do you know how humiliating it is at my age to get all red in the face at every little thing?"

"Every little thing?" He sounded amused. "I must have lost my touch if that's what you call it."

He was teasing her just the way he used to. If the subject had been anything else, she'd have welcomed this return to the old ways. But the feelings he'd awakened in her were too new and too astonishing to joke about.

He must be aware of how unsure she felt, how much out of her depth she was. Proudly she raised her chin and looked him in the eye. "You know what I mean—"

An enormous crash from below made her jump and cry out. "Omigosh, he's hurt himself!"

When she would have rushed past him toward the stairs, Boone caught her arm. "More likely he flung that vase of roses against the door. I'll go check while you—" his appreciative glance roamed pointedly down her satin length "—slip into something more comfortable."

Long after he'd taken the cane and departed, she stood in the deepening shadows trying to come to terms with what had just happened between them. Could she still have special feelings for Daniel Boone Taggart?

After Boone had gone away to law school, things were never the same. Two years after he left, she graduated from high school. Thom T. sent her to college to earn her nursing degree, and that's where she was when her mother died.

Eileen was buried in the Taggart family plot here on the Rocking T. Boone had come for the funeral; she remembered the comfort she took in the warm clasp of his hand, and the quick hug of farewell that came too soon.

The Rocking T had always been home base to her, still was, even without Boone or Jesse here. Aunt June retired and moved to Florida, but Kit kept coming back to the ranch every chance she got. Thom T. was her rock, the one constant in her life. She put all thoughts of Boone behind her, even managing to feel a trifle superior when she heard of his professional success with some big law firm. Superior—because she knew he was giving up more than he could possibly gain.

He obviously didn't appreciate the most important things in life—things like family and roots and *love.* She showed her growing disdain by avoiding the ranch when she knew he would be there. But he returned less and less frequently, and then he transferred to his firm's London office and for a long time didn't come back to Texas at all.

In the meantime, Kit had grown even closer to Thom T., regarding him as her only family. She owed him so much, more than she could ever repay.

Thom T. is everything to me, she thought, slipping out of the gown. *I can't let Boone turn my head with a few kisses.* What was the test of love, anyway? She'd always thought it was putting the welfare of another before her own. By that yardstick or any other, she loved the crusty old man.

Nobody's going to hurt him while I'm here, not even his own grandson, she vowed, hurrying down the attic stairs. But in her heart of hearts, she never for a moment thought Boone was trying to get around her with a few kisses, no matter how powerfully they rocked her world.

He was simply too honorable a man for that. Like her, he'd been caught up in a moment of crazy magic. But real life wasn't like that.

Of course not.

"KING ME," Thom T. demanded, an evil grin transforming his weathered features. "You can give up now if you wanna."

Kit made a face. "How come you always get the black checkers and make me take red?" she groused. "I always lose with the red."

"Ha! You always lose, period. Ready to holler uncle?"

Considering that he had four kings and three men left and she had one king with his back to the wall and one other measly little man, she might as well. She shoved all the playing pieces to the middle of the board. "I'll concede a draw."

Thom T. cackled. "In your dreams, baby girl, in your dreams." He settled back in his chair on the porch, his cast extended on a stool. "So, did you get a kick outta all that old stuff in the attic? Find anything interestin' molderin' away up there?"

"Lots." Kit began to replace the checkers in their carrying case. "Nothing that specifically sheds light on the legend of Showdown, though. I didn't get through a fraction of what's there, of course."

He nodded. "Buncha junk, mostly." But he didn't say that as if he really considered it junk.

"I did find one thing I'd like to talk to you about. It's the wedding gown—"

Boone walked into the room and Kit forgot what she was about to say. Which was just as well because Thom T.'s focus changed entirely.

"Boone-boy, how's about a quick game a' checkers with your pore old aged grandpa?" Thom T. wheedled.

Boone looked wonderful even in his dude sportswear. His skin glowed damp from the shower and his wet hair gleamed. When he passed Kit, she caught a whiff of some elegant after-shave. She swallowed hard and worked on keeping her expression vague.

"Pore old aged grandpa my—" Boone looked quickly at Kit "—Aunt Petunia! You've been a checker hustler all your life, and you're older than God."

Thom T. gave an exaggerated sigh, but his eyes sparkled with pleasure at Boone's friendly teasing. "You got that right." He pointed to a chair. "Set yourself." He twisted toward Kit. "Now what was it you wanted to talk about, hon?"

Kit glanced at Boone and saw veiled interest in his eyes. For some reason, she felt self-conscious asking Thom T. for a favor with Boone present. "N-nothing," she said. "It was nothing."

Thom T. frowned. "Now, Kitty..."

"She wants to borrow that old wedding gown she found up there in the attic," Boone said, his eyes narrowing shrewdly. "For Showdown Days."

Kit's mouth fell open. "How on earth did you know?"

Boone shrugged. "Magic," he said.

Kit felt the blush begin in her throat and rise to flame in her cheeks.

"Now, don't get riled," Thom T. instructed, apparently mistaking the cause of her distress. "I don't even know which dress you're talkin' about."

"Great-great-Grandmother Diana's," Boone said. "We've got a picture around somewhere of her wearing it."

"I'm astonished you'd recognize a dress from merely seeing a photo of it," Kit said. "I'd be amazed at *any* man who remembered a dress."

Boone smiled. "In my line of work a good memory is essential, and details count."

Thom T. looked from one of them to the other, frowning. "You wanna wear that dress when you play my great-aunt Rose in the big whoopty-do comin' up?" he asked Kit.

"It was just a thought." She tried to weasel out of what she'd started. "I realize it's too old and too precious to risk. Forget I mentioned it."

"Hogwash."

That evaluation came from Boone, not from Thom T. The old man and Kit both looked at him in surprise.

Boone spread his hands. "Just my opinion," he said. "If you could see how she looks in it, you'd let her have it in a minute." He shrugged expressively.

Kit stifled a groan. Now he'd told Thom T. she'd already tried on the dress. Not that the old man was likely to mind, but she didn't particularly enjoy having everyone in the household know she'd overstepped the bounds of propriety.

"Don't matter how she looks in it," Thom T. declared.

Boone frowned. "Have a heart, Thom T.," he said, more an order than a plea. "She's determined to wear it—"

"I am not!" Aghast, Kit tossed in her two cents' worth. "It's just that the *old* pageant wedding dress was ruined last year and we need to find another one." She glared at Boone. "I just thought—"

"You don't have to explain. I'm on your side," Boone protested.

She didn't want him on her side; it was too dangerous to her mental health. "It was a bad idea," she declared. "The gown's too small—I couldn't even get it fastened around my waist."

"I didn't notice," Boone lied smoothly, his eyes dancing with mischief. "Maybe I'm not as hot on details as I thought."

Kit was sure that every freckle on her face must be glowing with mortification. Thom T. cleared his throat pointedly, and she twisted around, grateful for the interruption.

"What I *meant* to say was, don't matter how she looks in it 'cause far's I'm concerned, if she wants it, she's got it, and that's that."

Kit's heart leapt with pleasure. But she had to be sure she hadn't finagled him into anything. "Thom T., are you sure?"

"You tryin' to *in*sult me, girl? I look like I ain't in my right mind?"

She had to laugh at that. "You old faker," she accused. "Thank you. I'll be careful with it, I promise."

"Good," he said, "because I'm hopin' someday ol' Boone here'll marry a gal who'll come down the aisle wearin' it. If Meg an' Jesse hadn't eloped, I'd have talked her into it sure. Then Rachel and Trey tied the knot, but she's too blasted tall. Now it's all up to Boone...."

As the old man talked on, Kit's glance met Boone's and held for a moment before he looked away almost...uneasily. In a flash, she realized that any understanding that might have been cautiously building between them had been swept aside. As had her joy at the prospect of wearing the gown.

Every time she touched it now, she would be looking into the future and seeing some fancy Eastern woman wearing the wedding gown for real, not for playing dressup. And Boone's future bride would doubtless be skinny enough to button it without difficulty, too.

Gritting her teeth, Kit promised herself she'd dig through the attic for a corset. Between that and a crash diet, she'd have the smallest waist in three counties by the time Showdown Days rolled around.

Thom T. and Boone had moved on to other topics. Kit stood up and when they glanced her way, explained, "Meeting for Showdown Days. Thanks so much for loaning us the wedding gown, Thom T. Everybody'll be tickled to death."

"Aw, get along with you!" He waved her gratitude aside. "Help yourself to anything you find up there."

"I'll take you up on that."

"Wait a minute." Boone stood. "There's something I need to talk to you about before you go, Kit. I'll walk out with you."

A prickle of unwanted excitement touched her spine. "Can't it wait?" She looked at her watch. "If I don't hurry I'll be late."

He cocked his head to one side. "What are they going to do—start without you? You're the star."

The telephone rang and Thom T. picked it up.

"I'm one of the stars," Kit admitted self-consciously. "But I'd never dream of keeping anyone waiting."

"It's fer you, Boone." Thom T. held out the receiver.

Boone took it. "I've been expecting this call." He covered the mouthpiece with one hand. "I'll just be a minute, Kit—"

She was shaking her head before he even finished speaking. "Sorry, but I've got to run. Maybe when I get back. I won't be late."

"Damn it, you'll regret it if you don't give me a chance to—"

A sudden and bone-deep premonition swept over her. "Not now, Boone. Some other time."

She walked out of the room and out of the house and climbed into her little economy car. Hand trembling, she tried to get the key into the ignition. Whatever Boone wanted to say to her she was absolutely certain she didn't want to hear.

RITA, OF COURSE, was delighted about the loan of the wedding gown. "That'll give us time to round up a permanent replacement for next year," she said. "Always assuming we survive *this* year."

Kit could understand her reservations. Usually by June, the entire celebration was long since set. This year, due to circumstances beyond anybody's control, everything was still up in the air.

Scanning the crowded meeting room, she chose a seat next to a pretty blonde with a California tan. "Hi," Kit said, smiling. "I don't think we've met. I'm Kit Mc-Crae."

"Oh, Rose Taggart—my sister-in-law." The blonde offered her hand and a grin. "I'm Chelsea Merton—or Diana Taggart to my many fans."

"That's great!" Kit settled back in her chair. She judged the other woman to be in her early twenties, and her accent, or lack of same, gave her away. "How'd you get involved in this extravaganza, Chelsea? You're obviously not from around here."

Chelsea wrinkled her nose. "Gosh, how'd you guess?" She laughed. "Actually, I'm from California. I'm just visiting my aunt Jenny for the summer. Maybe you know her—Jenny Merton?"

"Everybody knows Jenny."

"So I'm finding out. She's the one who told me I should get involved with Showdown Days, but she didn't warn me what a big deal it was," Chelsea said, somewhat apprehensively. "I'm feeling a little bit out of place with all you Texans. With my accent, I'm afraid I'll stick out like a sore thumb."

"That's the beauty of it—Diana wasn't a Texan. She came from back East and ended up marrying a Taggart and settling down in Showdown, or Jones, as it was called then."

Chelsea's brown eyes widened. "Wow, you're really up on your local history. Do you know the Taggarts? Aunt Jenny says some of them are still living around here but probably won't be much longer."

Her words, true though they might be, were like a knife thrust to Kit's heart. "Thom T. Taggart *is* getting old, but he has two grandsons. And one of them might...might decide to carry on the family traditions."

"Aunt Jenny says one is married and has his own ranch, and the other lives in New York and doesn't care anything at all about the old ways." Chelsea, obviously unaware of the pain her words might cause her listener, winked. "But she says he's cute enough to make up for it. What she actually said is that he's—now let me get this right—cute as a little speckled pup!"

"That's about it," Kit agreed, eager to change the subject. "As a matter of fact, I've lived out at the Rocking T since I was just a kid, so I've always had a special interest in the Taggarts and their part in the legend of Showdown."

"That's great. Maybe—"

Rita called for order, and the two young women obediently turned their attention to the stage of the community building. Rita passed out copies of the Showdown Days schedule, which would begin on a Sunday and conclude the following Saturday—a full week of activities that challenged the entire town but was especially grueling for the principal players.

The celebration would begin slowly, as was the custom. The heart of downtown would be cordoned off, and no mechanized vehicles allowed for the duration of the festivities. Everyone was encouraged to wear period dress, but for local businessmen, and especially townspeople who'd been assigned parts, costumes were mandatory.

Rita banged her gavel again. "No big changes or surprises here," she declared, waving her clipboard. "Major events begin with the quilting bee—quilting ladies, remember that the quilt must be finished by Friday so it can be raffled off. Every spare minute you have, I want to see those needles flying!"

Ruby Brown flashed a thumbs-up. "In that amount of time, I could make the quilt all by my lonesome," she declared.

Everyone nodded and murmured approval; Ruby Brown could back up her brag. She always won quilting prizes at the fair and was an acknowledged master of the art.

"That's great, Ruby." Rita consulted her schedule. "Also on Monday we have the first real biggie—Boone, the Mysterious Gunfighter, rides into town. He sees Rose—" Rita looked pointedly at Kit "—he's smitten, he makes a pest of himself, et cetera et cetera." She shuffled pages impatiently. "Then on Tuesday we have the horse race on Main Street, which will of course be won by Sheriff Jack, who'll claim a winner's kiss from—"

"Wait a minute!" Chelsea held up her hand. "Am I the only one here who doesn't really know what this legend is all about?" She glanced around, inquiry on her face.

Rita sighed. "Right now I've got too much to cover to get into that. You'll catch on as we go along, and what you don't understand, I promise somebody'll explain later, okay?"

"I guess so." Chelsea settled back into her seat.

"Good. Now, as I was about to say, on Tuesday we have the horse race on Main Street, and Boone pursues Rose."

A hiss greeted this announcement and Rita grinned. "Hey, the show's only as good as the villain. Right, Harry?" She looked around in alarm. "Harry? Where are you?"

"He was here earlier," a voice called.

Chelsea nudged Kit's elbow. "Who's Harry?"

"Harry Meeks. He's playing Boone, the Mysterious Gunfighter." Where *was* Harry? Rita was right; without a strong villain the show simply wouldn't work.

"Yawl lookin' for me?"

At the sound of Harry's mild voice, everyone swung toward the door. There stood Harry Meeks, every bit the Southern gentleman, not at all the scruffy gunfighter.

"You're kidding!" Chelsea gave Kit an incredulous glance.

I wish, Kit thought. "He'll look more dangerous when we get him roughed up a little around the edges," she said hopefully.

"I don't think he's *got* edges."

"Trust me." Staring at Harry, Kit's uneasiness grew. What was Rita thinking of? "He's a quick study and we don't have a lot of time this year," she added defensively. "Harry'll be fine."

Chelsea did not seem convinced.

"On Wednesday," Rita continued, "Boone punches out Rose's brother, James, and Rose tracks the dastard down in the saloon and slaps his face."

"My favorite part," crowed Bud Williams, whose role as Sheriff Jack gave him considerable leeway for swaggering. He was, after all, the hero of the piece.

Rita quelled him with a glance. "Also on Wednesday we have the showing of *The Legend of Texas Rose.*"

"What showing?" Chelsea whispered.

"Silent movie—1925," Kit whispered in reply.

"On Thursday Boone's gang rides into town and they throw their weight around. Later that same day Sheriff Jack proposes and Rose accepts."

Bud laughed and half stood to peer over the heads of the crowd. "Hear that, Kit? You gotta accept whether you want to or not! Cain't mess with history."

"No," Rita shot back, "and you can't mess with my actress, either!"

Catcalls and hoots of laughter greeted this pronouncement, all of which Bud took with good grace. "But I get t' kiss her, right?" he persisted.

"You know you do," Rita conceded, irritation in her voice.

"Famous first!" someone from the ranks shouted, and everyone dissolved into laughter. Bud's pursuit of Kit, and every other pretty girl in Showdown, was well known.

"Come to order, people! We've got a lot of ground to cover here." Rita waited for silence, then continued. "Since Thursday is also the Fourth of July, we'll have a big fireworks display that night. The barn dance and fight are on Friday, and I don't want anybody getting hurt this year."

"Somebody got hurt last year?" Chelsea asked out of the side of her mouth.

"Somebody gets hurt every year," Kit answered likewise. "Nothing serious. A few black eyes and mild concussions—nothing to write home about."

Chelsea gave her companion an incredulous glance, but Rita was still speaking.

"...for the big shoot-out Saturday. Harry and Bud, you'll have to put in extra rehearsal time to get it right. Okay?"

"Don't worry," Bud said. "I been practicin' my fast draw, Rita. I can take him fair and square."

Rita rolled her eyes. "What, me worry?" She turned toward Harry. "How about you? We'll have to work out a schedule for you and Bud...." Her voice trailed off and she frowned. "What is it now, Harry?"

Harry slumped in the back row. "I don't know about this, Rita. I said I'd do it, but...yawl wouldn't hurt my feelin's if you got somebody else." He shifted around as if appealing to the crowd. "I saw Boone Taggart the other day. Couldn't he...?"

A collective groan arose. Rita planted her hands on her hips. "Harry, Boone won't do it. I've asked him. Others have asked him. Did you ask him?"

"Well...yes."

"And he said...?"

"No. But what if I could get him to change his mind?"

Rita spoke clearly and distinctly. "Harry, if you can get Boone to change his mind, more power to you. But in the meantime, *you said you'd do it and you're stuck with the part.*"

Chelsea shifted, one hand shielding her mouth while she whispered in Kit's ear. "They want some local guy named Boone to play the guy in the play named Boone? Now I'm really confused."

No more confused than I am, Kit thought later on the drive back to the ranch. Showdown Days was a shambles, but so were her emotions. Ever since Boone kissed her, first in the corral and then in the attic, she'd thought of little else. She was edging closer and closer to admitting that there was just the faintest possibility that she might still be . . . in love with Daniel Boone Taggart.

Wouldn't it be wonderful if he relented and decided to stay around for a while? If he agreed to become a part of Showdown Days? He could be Sheriff Jack, the hero; he'd done it before and he'd been wonderful. Or he could be the villain—whatever he wanted. Either way, she as Rose would work with him, play with him.

Either way, he would kiss her again, hold her in his arms.

She climbed out of her car and entered the house quietly, in case Thom T. was already in bed. Lights glowed from the parlor to the left of the big entry hall, but she headed past, toward the stairs and her own room.

"Kit?"

She stopped, the hairs at the nape of her neck prickling a warning. Boone's voice, deadly serious . . . She spun around to face him. "What is it?"

"Could you come in here for just a minute?" He indicated the parlor.

Her heart stood still. "Is Thom T. all right?" she whispered.

Boone's implacable expression didn't change. "He's fine. Please." He gestured for her to precede him.

She entered reluctantly. She hated this feeling of impending doom; she'd had it all evening and hadn't been able to shake it off. Now, Boone's demeanor intensified her nameless fears.

"What is it?" she asked, her glance finding Thom T. He sat in his wheelchair, his leathery face as serious as his grandson's.

"Sit down first," Boone suggested, indicating the brocaded Victorian sofa.

"Darn it!" Kit's temper flared and she stamped one foot. "You're scaring me! Will the two of you kindly tell me what's going on here?"

"I wanted to prepare you for this eventuality earlier, but no, you were in too big a hurry," Boone accused.

"Prepare me for what? If you're trying to tell me you've decided to go back to New York, believe me, I can take it!"

"Yellin' won't help," Thom T. interjected. He sounded tired and looked discouraged.

Boone, concentrating on Kit, didn't even seem to hear his grandfather. "You tryin' to say you want me to leave?" he demanded of her, Texas making a strong resurgence in his speech. "'Cause if you are, I flat don't believe it."

Kit tossed her head. "Why should I want you around? With your superior airs and high-hat manners—"

"The hell you say!" Boone's tightly controlled mask slipped entirely, and his lips pulled back over even white teeth. "I could make you eat those words."

"Boone, Kit—"

She ignored the old man's effort to stem the angry tide. "You are—you're conceited and spoiled, Daniel Boone Taggart. You come back here once in a blue moon, like you own everything and everybody, and start throwing your weight around. You say, 'Jump,' and we're supposed to ask, 'How high?' Well, I won't!"

His face flushed darkly and he took a menacing step toward her. She was getting to him. Rightly or wrongly, she could see she was getting to him.

She took a perverse delight in the erosion of his control. "Just because you're bigger and stronger, you think you can have everything your own way—"

"Shut up," he said in a tight voice.

"I won't! And you can't make me!" She lifted her chin and dared him.

"Oh, can't I?"

His angry gaze locked with hers, then slowly lowered to center on her trembling mouth. She caught her breath, unconsciously touching the tip of her tongue to her bottom lip. Realizing what she was doing, she snapped her mouth closed and whirled away.

He stopped her flight with his hands on her shoulders, pulling her back until her shoulder blades barely touched his chest. She felt his breath stir the curly tendrils of hair near her ear and fought down a groan.

"I don't have to depend on superior strength or size," he murmured, "and we both know it. I can prove that right here and now, but it might come as a shock to a man Thom T.'s age—"

"Gol dang it, you two young heathens get aholt of yourselfs afore I go cut me a hickory switch!"

She felt Boone's fingers tightening convulsively. Then his hands fell away. Turning quickly, she faced the angry old man in the wheelchair, her heart in her throat.

He wasn't looking at her; he was glowering at his grandson. "Tell her," Thom T. ordered. "Tell her what you told me and do it now."

CHAPTER SIX

"THERE'S BEEN a good offer for the ranch. I think Thom T. should take it."

Boone's stark declaration took Kit's breath away. This was her worst nightmare come true. She had tried to make herself believe that the longer Boone spent on the ranch the more he'd remember his roots. Instead, he'd been busy lining up buyers—buyers for her heart and Thom T.'s soul.

"But... what? How?" Angry and confused, she beseeched the old man sitting in the wheelchair. "Thom T., don't let him do this to us!"

Thom T. looked aeons older than when she'd left a few hours earlier. She dropped to her knees beside him. Grasping his hands, she looked up into his weary face and was filled with a new worry. "Are you all right?"

He sighed. She could count on the fingers of one hand the times she'd seen this man without a glint in his eyes, but this was one of those times.

"I been better," he admitted. He squeezed her hands, then pushed them away. "I'm wore to a frazzle. I gotta get me some shut-eye, but I couldn't go to bed without you knowin'. I didn't want you thinkin' we'd keep anything this important from you."

Still kneeling, she rocked back on her heels. "Surely that doesn't mean you're going to sell!"

"It means—" he gave a disgusted snort "—it means I'm gonna *think* about it, and that's the only promise I can make."

Kit darted Boone an accusing glare, which Thom T. saw.

"Now, don't go for each other's throats again," he warned. "I know yawl both think you're right, but there's two sides to ever' story."

He shook his silver head. "Kit, Taggart-born women been scarce as hen's teeth in this family for generations, but you been a daughter *and* a granddaughter to me. I'd cut off my right arm before I'd let you down."

"I. . . ." She stared at him, unable to go on while tears welled in her eyes.

He patted her shoulder awkwardly. "I know you're tryin' to look out for my interests, but I gotta remind you that I've been around long enough to know how to take care of myself. I gotta look at the big pitcher here."

He turned to his grandson. "And you, Dan'l Boone, I know you're doin' what you're doin' outta love."

"Ah, Grandpa . . ."

Boone sounded so miserable that Kit looked up at him in surprise. His chin was on his chest and his eyes were gray and stormy.

"But I gotta say to the both a'yawl—" Thom T. leaned back, frowning "—gimme some rope. I got serious thinkin' to do. When I decide what's what, yawl will be the first to know. 'Nough said?"

Not nearly enough for Kit. But he'd made his wishes clear and she'd try her best not to go against them. Sneaking another glance at Boone's unhappy expression, she wondered if he would also put the old man first. She supposed she'd soon find out.

FORTY MINUTES LATER, Kit joined Boone in the kitchen. They'd got Thom T. settled for the night, then parted without another word. She'd prepared for bed, at the last minute throwing a light cotton robe over her summer nightgown. She needed a snack—or so she'd told herself.

Boone's story appeared to be identical, with the exception that he really *did* want something to eat, judging from the enormous wedge of apple pie in front of him. He wore a thick white terry-cloth robe, and his strong brown legs stuck out beneath the small kitchen table. Kit found herself wondering what he had on under the robe and then berated herself for such a thought.

Drops of moisture clung to his hair and sparkled in the bright kitchen lighting. He gave her a quick glance and then went back to his pie, his expression unreadable.

She fired the opening salvo. "That was a dirty trick." She opened the refrigerator door and peered inside.

"What was?"

"Waiting until I left tonight to tell Thom T. about this so-called offer."

He finished the pie and laid his fork beside his plate, lining it up carefully with the table edge. "This so-called offer came in just as you were leaving. I tried to get you to hang around so we could talk, if you recall."

She pulled out a jug of orange juice. "As I recall, you asked me to hang around *before* the call came in. Get your story straight before you try to sell it, Boone."

"Not necessary when you're telling the truth," he inserted smoothly. "This deal has been in the works for several days now. I wanted to give you a little advance warning, that's all. I didn't know exactly when it'd come to a head—I didn't really expect it so soon—but I knew it was coming."

"Thanks for nothing." She took a gulp of orange juice; it was so sour it puckered her mouth. Funny, it'd tasted fine at breakfast. "So, who is it? Somebody who wants to open a dude ranch?"

"No."

"Not wildcatters!"

He shook his head.

"Who, then?" she cried, exasperated. "No doubt somebody out to rape the land one way or the other."

"That's a big part of your trouble, Kit—you're always sure. And more often than not, you're wrong."

She banged her empty glass down on the table. How'd he always manage to get her so worked up while he remained calm? It gave him an unfair advantage, but she didn't seem to be able to help herself. "Are you going to tell me who the low-life, low-down back stabber is or not?" She forced the words from between gritted teeth.

"Of course, when you ask so prettily." He said the last word with mocking emphasis. "It's a cattle company from west Texas. They want to restore the Rocking T to its former glory as a working ranch."

She flung back her head, her voice rising defensively. "This *is* a working ranch! Thom T. has horses, cattle. How dare you imply this is nothing more than a...a hobby!"

The minute the word was out of her mouth she regretted it, for that was exactly what the Rocking T had become: an old man's hobby run by part-time cowboys. Tears burned her eyes as she blinked furiously, refusing to be humbled before Boone.

He leaned his forearms on the table and laced his fingers. "Be reasonable, Kit. This is the perfect solution. Thom T. can walk away with a clear conscience, knowing he won't be letting down the land or the town or anybody else. I want to take him back East with me, set him up nearby—Connecticut, maybe—where I can keep an eye on him."

He looked so sanctimonious sitting there, laying out his plans without regard for the feelings of anyone else. She clenched her hands into fists. "Turncoat," she threw at him. "You just want to soothe your conscience, because you've neglected him all these years."

He flinched and the lines around his mouth turned white. Sparks that could be anger leapt into his eyes. "Katherine McCrae," he said, each word distinct and menacing, "I've never neglected my responsibilities, or my grandfather. Who do you think's been handling the family oil interests all these years? Who do you think—"

He stopped and drew a breath, which seemed to settle him. His eyes narrowed. "I've tried to be sensitive to your feelings," he said in his calm lawyer's voice, "but this is Taggart family business and none of your own."

LYING IN BED that night, Kit couldn't deny that his final words had crushed her. It was impossible to stop replaying the scene in her mind; the hurt just wouldn't go away. "Taggart family business," he'd said, and none of her own.

Thom T. is my family, she comforted herself, *no matter what Boone thinks.*

But Boone was Taggart flesh and blood while she…she was no one in particular. And he was totally indifferent to her opinion on the subject of Thom T.'s welfare.

Only as she drifted on the edge of troubled sleep did she remember the way he'd flinched when she'd called him a turncoat.

BOONE WAS GONE by the time Kit rose the next morning. He'd helped Thom T. up, fixed the old man's breakfast, got him settled on the glass-enclosed porch and then driven away.

"Back to New York?" Kit mumbled, rubbing eyes that felt like corduroy. She hoped he had, because she never wanted to see his face again; she prayed he hadn't, because nothing was settled, at least as far as she was concerned.

"Naw," Thom T. said. "San Antonio, more like. Forget him—I got some tall thinkin' to do, girl. Could I get you to drive me around the place today? I always think better when I get away from civilization." He shuddered as if hemmed in by his own house.

Kit didn't need convincing. She, too, needed to do some serious thinking.

KIT DROVE Thom T.'s big Cadillac beneath the shade of a stand of oak trees at the edge of a pasture. Pressing a button, she lowered the windows before turning off the engine. The day lay around them hot and humid, but a faint breeze stirred here in the shade. For a moment she and Thom T. sat in silence.

He was first to speak. "There they come," he declared with obvious satisfaction, pointing. Sure enough, white-faced cattle drifted toward the automobile. "Cow-critters may be dumb, but they're among the most curious beasts on God's green earth," he said musingly.

She shifted on the seat, more interested in him than in the animals. She thought she saw almost a hunger in his face when he looked at his land and his small herd. For the hundredth time, she wondered what he would do shut up in a house back East.

"That skinny heifer over there's limpin'," he said suddenly.

Kit glanced at the cows, six or eight of them surrounding the car. "I don't see a skinny heifer."

Thom T. pointed to a cow that looked identical to all the others, at least to Kit. "That one there. I'll hav'ta call Doc Wagner, get him out here to take a look-see. Might even lure him into a game of checkers."

"I'll call him for you, Thom T."

He gave her a sharp glance. "I ain't helpless. I'll do it."

Startled by his barbed tone, she settled back. The stock was fat and frisky, but there were so few—no more than a dozen in this small herd. The word "hobby" sprang to mind.

"Sorry I came down so hard on you, gal."

His rueful tone surprised her. "That's okay," she said. "I know you're under a lot of pressure."

"Ain't no excuse."

He looked away and she saw him in profile, his features still strong and well-defined despite his advanced years. "How old are you, Thom T.?" she found herself asking.

"I was born in 1908, the same year as the Model T Ford. I'm still here but it ain't." He chuckled and relaxed against the plush leather seat. The humor faded and a melancholy expression took its place. "I was born right here on this land. So was my boys."

"Travis, Jesse and Daniel," Kit supplied.

He cast her a curious glance. "That's right. Seems like you know a lot about the Taggarts."

"Not nearly as much as I'd like to." She wrapped one hand around the steering wheel. "I know your sons are all . . . gone, but I don't know what happened."

Thom T. gave a gusty sigh. "Jesse died in Korea and Dan'l got kilt ridin' a motorcycle. Travis..."

"Boone and Jesse's father?"

"That's right. Throwed by a hoss in '72, drug to death right here on the Rocking T. The boys' ma, Shirley, passed away a couple years earlier." Thom T.'s attention focused at some point on the horizon. "Travis's the one took over the awl bidness when my brother, Dan'l, cashed in his chips."

Oil business, Kit mentally translated. "I'm sorry," she said, feeling inadequate to soften old tragedies.

"No need, baby girl. It was a long time ago. Dan'l never married but—boy, howdy!—did he ever know how to make money!"

One fat cow grazed so close to the open car window that Kit reached through without thinking and patted its flank. With a startled glance of big brown eyes, the cow went back to cropping grass. "Will you tell me about your father, Thom T.?"

A broad grin split the leathery face. "He was a corker, that one. Boone's named for him, y'know. He was born along about 1876. Spent his whole life on this ranch—'ceptin' when my ma would devil him into takin' her to the big city." He shook his head in open admiration. "Pa us'ta say there was no place on earth like Texas and the Rocking T. I believed him."

"Who started it all? Who was the first Texas Taggart?"

He thought for a moment. "Well," he began slowly, "I guess that'd be my great-great-grandpa Thomas...."

Thomas Taggart came to Texas from Tennessee in 1821 with a wife and two-year-old son; his second son, Jesse Daniel, called J.D., was born days after the family arrived. Thomas was one of fifty-nine Texans who drafted and sighed the Texas declaration of independence from

Mexico in 1836, and he died in a skirmish with Mexican troops not long after. The oldest son, James, died at the Alamo; J.D., although no more than a boy, also fought for Texas independence and survived without a scratch.

"Them was the days," Thom T. said with fervor, "when a man would fight for what he believed in—die for it, too, if'n need be. 'Remember the Alamo' was more than a snappy slogan designed to sell a hamburger or some such. It meant, 'Remember the men who stood up for what they believed—Jim Bowie, William Barret Travis, Davy Crockett . . . and James Taggart, too.'"

He twisted toward her, his eyes glowing. "Taggarts fought ol' Santy Anny and they fought Comanches and Apaches and sometimes they fought each other. But mostly they fought for the land—first that little ol' place on Handbasket Creek where Jesse and Meg have staked their claim, and then for the Rocking T.

"My great-grandpa, Jesse Daniel, was a ripsnorter from what my pa told me. He was a rancher, and when he got back from the war—"

"The War between the States?"

"That's the one. When he come home, ever'thin' had gone plumb to h—" He gave her a sheepish grin. "Gone to hades. Cows took to the brush, horses stole or wandered, no crops, kids runnin' wild. . . ."

"James and Rose?"

"That's right, my grandpa James and my great-aunt Rose, them two that Showdown Days is about. Neither one a' them was ten year old when the war hit. James did a man's job of work, though, tryin' to hold things together with his ma. Showdown—Jones, they called the town then—didn't see any war action, but a lotta local men got kilt one side or th' other." He grinned. "Great-grandpa J.D. got a medal. Might be up there somewhere in the attic. Grandpa James said he never did talk about it much.

"Anyway, after the war Great-grandpa started trailin' herds north. At first they went to Missouri, but the railroads kept pushin' farther and farther west and Kansas was the place—boy, howdy!" He gave Kit a crooked grin. "I always been sorry I missed them days."

"It must have been exciting. Did your grandfather James ever go on the trail drives himself?"

"Lordy, yes!"

"But he didn't go in 1876, the summer the Mysterious Gunfighter Boone came to town?"

"Grandpa said he stayed home because he had a broken arm. His pa went, instead—made Grandpa madder than a wet hen. He was practically a newlywed at the time, but it hurt his pride to stay home. I reckon he was afraid somebody'd think he was henpecked, tied to Grandma Diana's apron strings. I was just a pup when he died, but I remember him tellin' stories."

Kit's eyes widened. "I didn't know that—I mean, a broken arm sure isn't taken into account during the Showdown Days celebration. That gunfighter must have been even worse than we know, to beat up a man with a broken arm."

Thom T. lifted his busy white brows. "Makes no never mind," he said mildly. "That ain't the only *mis*representation of historical fact perpetrated by Showdown Days."

"But we—everybody's always tried so hard to make it accurate," Kit protested. "Ever since the beginning—"

"Which was forty years ago or better, tales told by other than Taggarts," he reminded her.

"But...." What was he getting at? "Did your grandfather ever tell you what *really* happened that summer the gunfighter came to town?"

"Nope, and I never asked him, because nobody in the family wanted to talk about my great-aunt Rose. It was nothin' to be proud of, causin' a gunfight." He laughed. "It only got to be somethin' to be proud of later."

"Then, are you saying you don't believe the legend is true?" Kit asked slowly, dread a leaden lump in her stomach.

"A hundred-percent true? Kitty-gal, ain't hardly nothin' on this earth that's a hundred-percent true. What difference does it make—hundred-percent, ten-percent—long as ever'body's happy?"

"I guess you're right," she said, but she didn't really mean it. She *wanted* the legend to be one hundred-percent true; she wanted absolutes. She was one-hundred-percent right about what was best for Thom T. and the Rocking T, and she wanted Boone to be one-hundred-percent wrong.

Boone. That brought up another question. "Thom T., was your grandmother Diana really kin to Daniel Boone?"

The old man chuckled. "Hard to say. If'n she weren't, that's one part a' the legend that fails to hold water. Why would my grandma name her firstborn after that gunfighter if he was the yella dog folks say he was? So she musta had Boones back there in her family tree someplace."

"That's got to be it," Kit agreed. "Nothing else makes sense."

"Nope. Nothing else makes sense." But his eyes twinkled when he said it.

KIT DROVE HIM NEXT to the little family graveyard on a hillock overlooking the ranch house. All the Taggarts were there: Jesse Daniel, born 1821, died 1888; James, born

1850, died 1920, resting beside his wife, Diana, and two children who did not survive to adulthood; their son Boone, who did—Thom T.'s father, born 1876 and died 1927, beside his wife, Martha; Thom T.'s beloved wife, Miss Aggie, laid to rest too young in 1935 at the tender age of twenty-six, leaving behind a bereft husband and three little boys.

Someday—please, Lord, not too soon, Kit thought— Thom T. would lie beside her. Unless the Rocking T passed out of Taggart control, of course. . . .

All three of Thom T.'s sons were buried in the family plot, along with Travis's wife, Shirley. Kit's mother's grave lay to one side, near the white picket fence that neatly delineated the boundaries of the small private cemetery beneath the sheltering arms of oak trees.

Watching Thom T. kneel to place an already wilting wildflower on his wife's grave, grief clutched Kit. Nearly a century and a half of Taggart history and the heart of an old man were tied up in this little piece of Texas. When Boone understood that, he would not—could not—pursue his diabolical plan.

OLD DOC WAGNER not only came over in late afternoon to examine the "skinny" heifer, he accepted Thom T.'s invitation to play checkers and argue politics afterward. Thus it was that Boone could say to Kit in an aside, "How about I buy you dinner at the Showdown Steak House? We've got to talk."

"Can't," she declined brusquely. "I've got a rehearsal at six. Besides, someone should stay here for Thom T."

Thom T. reared back in his wheelchair. "Dagnabit, girl! What'a you call Doc Wagner, a pinto pony?"

Doc grinned and continued arranging the checker-board. "I'm a-fixin' to clean this ol' boy's plow," he announced. "You young folks run along. I'll hang about until you get back."

Boone gave her an almost grin. "I'll get you to rehearsal on time," he promised.

She wasn't particularly eager to trust him, but she did need to talk to him. Once he knew how deep Thom T.'s feelings ran, surely Boone would back off from his cruel plan to sell the Rocking T. "Okay," she agreed reluctantly. "I'll ride into town with you, but I don't have time to eat. You'll just have to drop me off. Rachel will give me a lift home."

"Whatever you say, Miss Rose."

He made a mocking bow and opened the door for her. She swept past with her head at what she hoped was a queenly angle.

Driving onto the main road, he glanced at her. "You still mad?" he inquired.

She looked out the window. "I wasn't mad," she lied.

"Okay, disgusted." He looked for her reaction. "No? How about disappointed?"

"Disappointed." She said the word with distaste. "That's close enough." *Stop sparring with him,* she warned herself. *You'll catch more flies with honey.* "Boone..." She twisted around on the car seat and gazed at him beseechingly.

"Uh-oh." He sounded leery. "What're you up to now?"

"Me?" She touched her throat lightly with one hand, striving for sincerity. "I'm not up to a thing. But I do want to talk to you about... about the..."

He laughed deep in his chest. "*Sale,* Kitty. It's a four-letter word, but it's safe to say in polite company."

"Next time I'm in polite company—oops."

"Yeah, that's no way to butter me up," he agreed blandly. "What is it you want? Go on girl, spit it out."

He was beginning to sound more and more like old Boone, she realized with a pleasure she thrust swiftly aside. This was no time to be swayed by sentiment. "Well," she hedged, tracing the curve of the bucket seat with one finger, "I just thought . . . I mean, it occurred to me that since you've been gone for so long, maybe . . ."

He waited until it became apparent she'd floundered to a halt before he nudged gently, "Maybe what, hon?"

The easy endearment sent another rush of pleasure through her; she ignored it and hurried on. "Well, just that maybe you've forgotten how much the ranch means to your grandfather."

"I don't think so, but feel free to remind me," he invited.

She gulped. "I know I'm not a Taggart, so maybe I have no right. . . ."

"I'm sorry about that."

"What?"

"I've been ashamed of myself ever since I made that crack about your not being a Taggart. Damn, Kitty." He frowned straight ahead at the road. "You came here when you were practically a baby, and you've more or less been here ever since. I didn't mean to imply I thought you didn't have rights in this situation."

"Rights?" What on earth was he talking about? "I'm not interested in *rights*. I'm interested in your grandfather. I'm interested in preserving the history of a family I love—and envy!"

With the last word, she clapped one hand over her mouth, appalled at what she'd admitted. If he was a gentleman, he'd let it pass.

He wasn't and he didn't. "Envy? What's to envy?" He furrowed his brow. "The money?"

"No, not the money! Daniel Boone Taggart, you're an impossible man." Crossing her arms, she dropped back against her seat and exhaled sharply. "I wouldn't expect you to understand," she snapped. "You've always had family."

"You had family. You had your aunt June and your mother." He hesitated. "I don't believe I ever heard you mention your father."

"I wonder why?" Her voice dripped sarcasm. "Could it be because I'm not even sure who he was?"

"I'm sorry." He certainly sounded sympathetic, not shocked. "I didn't know."

"That's because you didn't ask," she retorted tartly. "It's not a secret. I just don't go around advertising it. At first I was ashamed, but then I realized nobody was really interested."

"That's not true."

He glanced at her, his handsome face open and appealing and filled with regret. Regret that he'd never taken the time to get to know her?

Embarrassed, she spoke quickly to distract him. "Doesn't matter." And it really didn't, not anymore. "Thom T. knew. He understood. I loved him for that, and for so much more." Tears pricked her eyelids and she steadied herself with a deep breath, continuing in a more controlled voice. "The day Aunt June picked me up at the bus station in San Antonio and drove me out to the Rocking T for the first time..."

"I remember," Boone said softly. "You were just a little bit of a thing."

"Down the steps came this ramrod-straight man with white hair, very intimidating. Two big boys were with him."

"Jesse and me."

"Yes. I wanted to turn and run. I probably would have if Aunt June hadn't stopped me."

Boone's voice became even softer. "Freckles and red hair and great big eyes. And scared."

"More scared than you can even imagine. And then Thom T. said, 'Welcome to the Rocking T,' in that drawl of his. I've loved him ever since. From that day forth, all you Taggarts have been my family, like it or not."

"We like it fine, Kitty."

She scooted around on the seat again, marshaling her courage. Maybe he would listen to her with his heart now. "Boone," she said with all the sincerity of which she was capable, "I'm not trying to cause trouble. I just want Thom T. to be happy—and you and Jesse and Meg, and Trey and Rachel, of course. But him especially—he loves the ranch, Boone, loves it. His history is buried in that little cemetery on the hill. Your history, too—someday soon that will matter to you. When it does, it should be there waiting for you."

He pulled into the lot beside the community center and into a parking space. Cutting the engine, he turned to her and took her hands in his.

She let out her breath in a gust of sound. "You do understand," she whispered.

He nodded. "Of course."

She saw him through a blur of tears. "And you won't sell the Rocking T out from under him?"

He looked affronted. "Certainly not."

"Oh, thank God." Her shoulders slumped in blessed relief. Maybe *she* had accomplished that miracle. Maybe bearing her soul to him as she'd done hadn't been the act of a crazed woman, after all. "W-when did you change your mind?"

Boone cocked his head to one side, frowning. "I didn't change my mind, Kitty. I never intended to sell the ranch out from under him—couldn't, as a matter of fact. He's got all his faculties. He's going to do it himself."

A vise closed around her throat. "But...but...you said you understood!"

"And I do. But I also understand that my grandfather is getting old. He should be with me, and my life is in New York."

In her agitation, she grabbed his shirt with both hands, the soft cotton knit stretching in all directions. "But your life could be here! Why do you want to live in that awful place? What do you have there that you couldn't have here, only better?"

And in a flash, she knew: a woman. The noise roaring in her ears was the sound of her own heart, breaking.

CHAPTER SEVEN

THERE SEEMED NOTHING left to say. Defeated, Kit tore at the car door, wanting only to escape.

But Boone caught her arm and held her there. "What's going on in that mind of yours?" he wondered out loud.

"I just figured out the mystery." She shook his hand away, unable to bear his touch a moment longer.

"What mystery?"

How could he sound so innocent? "The mystery of New York's appeal."

He looked amused. "This I've got to hear."

She tossed her head and glared at him. "Obviously it's a woman."

He gave her a blank look. "What woman?"

"The woman you're interested in."

"What makes you think I'm interested in a New York woman?"

"Your stubborn insistence on going back to that place, for one thing."

"Oh, I see. The fact that I work for a New York law firm and own a New York apartment doesn't count, I suppose. I couldn't just like it there?"

"Hardly." She arched a brow condescendingly.

"That evidence isn't even strong enough to be circumstantial. You'll have to do better. Give me one solid reason you think I've got some woman waiting in New York."

Meeting his gaze she said with soft scorn: *"Bree!"*

HE SAT THERE after Kit slammed the door behind her, trying to figure out how she had come up with that name. It took a while, but he finally remembered there'd been one telephone call. But surely...

Rita rounded the corner at a fast clip, heading toward the door to the community center. She saw Boone sitting in the car and came to an abrupt halt. "Are you here for the meeting?" she called hopefully.

He shook his head. She shrugged, gave him a last mournful glance and disappeared inside the building. Boone watched her go, but he was thinking of Bree. She hadn't exactly been on his mind lately, he realized.

That bothered him a little; he should have thought of her at least once in a while. There was no real commitment between them, but he'd figured that maybe one of these days...

Hell. A man couldn't think of a future with a woman whose face he didn't even remember after a week apart. Absence hadn't made his heart grow fonder; it was more a case of "out of sight, out of mind."

Thanks for pointing that out, Kit, he thought with irritation. *For a woman who doesn't want to cause anybody any trouble, you're doing a damned good job of it.*

Scowling, he climbed out of the car and stalked toward the community center door, completely ignoring the fact that he'd told everybody concerned he didn't want anything to do with Showdown Days.

KIT SAW HIM the moment he entered. Quickly she turned away so he wouldn't know she'd been watching for him. She was pleased that she'd taken a seat in the front row between Lee Cox and Chelsea—Rose's brother and sister-in-law, respectively.

Kit pasted a bright smile on her face for Chelsea, determined to make it crystal clear to Boone that she did not seek, or want, his attention.

Chelsea refused to cooperate. "*Who* is *that?*" she whispered, pointing.

"Nobody," Kit said. "Now about alterations to your costume—"

She knew he was behind her before he spoke, knew it by the way Chelsea's eyes widened. His voice sent little chills up Kit's spine. "Laddy," he said, "could I trouble you to change seats with me? Kit was supposed to save me a place, but she apparently forgot."

Kit whipped around, prepared to deny everything. Boone's quick smile brought her to a stuttering halt.

Lee rose. "Sure thing, Boone." He shifted one chair over. "But it's Lee now—nobody calls me Laddy anymore. You've been gone too long, man."

"You're not the first person to remark on that fact," Boone admitted dryly.

Lee grinned. "So you gonna participate in this extravaganza?"

Boone shook his head. "Not me. I'm just here to give Kit moral support. She's the star, you know." And he sat down, crossed his arms over his chest and looked at her expectantly.

Kit gritted her teeth. "Will you *please* go away and leave me alone?"

"No." He looked past her and saw Chelsea. "Hello," he said. "I'm Boone Taggart. I don't believe we've met."

"Chelsea Merton."

Kit, seated between them, tried to duck aside and, instead, moved directly into the path of Chelsea's hand.

Leaning back, she bumped into Boone's hand. Chelsea and Boone laughed, but it wasn't funny to Kit.

She jumped to her feet. "I seem to be in the way here," she exclaimed at the same moment Rita tapped on the podium for attention.

"Shall we get started? We've got a lot of ground to cover tonight." Rita shuffled through the papers on her clipboard. "I've got a few announcements to make, and then we'll break up for individual rehearsals. Townspeople, meet in the grade-school lunchroom. Barflies, gamblers and dance-hall girls will rehearse the big fight scene at the Yellow Rose Saloon, all except the principals, who'll be working right here in the community room—that's Rose, the sheriff, the gunfighter and the brother. Diana—where's my Diana?" Rita looked around the crowded room.

Chelsea waved her hand. "Here!"

"Diana, you and the quilting-bee ladies will go to the old church to rehearse the wedding scene. You can stand in for Rose."

"Okay," Chelsea agreed, then muttered under her breath, "Drat, I'll bet dance-hall girls have more fun!"

"Life isn't fair, is it," Kit agreed, tongue in cheek.

From the stage, Rita clapped her hands sharply. "All right, people, move!"

They did, scurrying in all directions until only the principals remained—the principals and Boone Taggart. Bud Williams approached and heaved his bulk onto the edge of the stage.

He looked slyly at Boone. "So, how's that big black Outlaw horse?" he inquired.

"Right as rain." Boone's reply was equally mild.

"I'm glad something is," Harry Meeks interjected. As always, he looked the very personification of a Southern gentleman with his light summer suit and his blue eyes and fair hair. "I'm not feelin' good about these rehearsals, not good at all. I don't know why I let yawl talk me into this. I'm just not comfortable playin' a bad man."

"Now, Harry—" Kit began, but Bud cut her off.

"You think *I* am?" Bud's beefy face reddened. "I been playin' that danged outlaw for the last three years—don't I deserve a break here? Three years in a row I been shot down on the street like a yella dog, and this time I wanna be the danged *survivor!*"

"I don't want your part, Bud," Harry denied. "I don't really want *any* part. I thought I did, but this is taking a lot more time than I can spare. Besides, somebody always gets hurt in the big fight scene, and this year it's bound to be me. Mother says—"

"Yawl ready to begin?" Rita approached the edge of the stage, taking in the situation at a glance. "Let's start with the proposal—Rose and Jack, up here, please."

"But I thought the fight scene was supposed to come first," Lee protested. "You said—"

Rita gave him an exasperated glance. "Doc Preston's off delivering a baby—I don't know why he considered that more important than coaching the fight scene. Don't worry, Lee, you'll get your chance to throw a few punches. In fact..." She cocked her head toward Boone, who'd been just an onlooker thus far. "Boone, suppose you could do me a favor?"

He leaned back in his seat. "Rita, I meant what I said about not—"

"I know, I know." She brushed aside his disclaimer. "I'm not asking you to play a part. But since you're here, it wouldn't hurt you any to help those who *are* willing to put themselves out a little for the good of the community— Sorry, that's no way to ask a favor, is it."

"Well, you did get my attention," Boone drawled, looking not the least bit offended. "You buttering me up for some special reason?"

Rita grinned. "Yep. How about workin' with Harry and Lee on their fight scene? Since you were in it once upon a time..."

"Glad to." Boone stood up with his customary grace. "All you had to do was ask." He turned toward his two pupils. "Why don't we find a quiet spot and talk this over?"

Good, Kit thought, watching them move away. *I'm nervous enough without having Boone watch me rehearse with Bud.* The future Sheriff Jack was proving to be a real handful without any outside encouragement.

Rita drew her two principals to the center of the stage. "Okay, Jack and Rose, you know the proposal will actually be made on the porch in front of the general store. We'll have microphones planted all around, so there shouldn't be any trouble with people hearing you. But please speak up just the same."

Bud-Jack hooked his thumbs through his belt loops and hitched up his jeans. "Like this?" he boomed.

Rita rolled her eyes and Kit stifled a giggle.

"Close enough," Rita said dryly. "Now, you both know what to do. Rose, you need to spend at least a half-hour shopping inside the store before the meeting with Jack. Come through the front door at two o'clock on the dot and—" she swung toward Bud "—you be there waiting for her. From the moment she goes inside, I want you loitering around, waiting for her to come back out. Play with the kids, pet dogs, help little old ladies across the street—whatever. Just make it clear you're waiting for Rose."

"I can do that," Bud agreed, all confidence. "I been waitin' *years* for Kit—I mean Rose." He guffawed.

Kit groaned. "Bud Williams, are you going to give me a hard time about this?" she demanded, planting her hands on her hips. "Because if you are—".

"Kit, please call him Jack," Rita intervened. "Start now or you'll never keep it straight when the time comes. Okay, pretend this is the door and you're walking out."

Rita stepped away and suddenly Kit found herself face-to-face with a grinning Bud-Jack. Quelling a moment's alarm, she smiled at him. "Why, it's Sheriff Jack," she said as flirtatiously as she could manage. "I do declare...."

Her attention skittered past him to settle across the room on Boone, who chose that moment to glance her way. He winked broadly, just as she opened her mouth to utter further social pleasantries. Her mind went blank and she stammered, "I, uh, what... you..."

"Howdy, Miz Rose," Bud-Jack boomed, obviously unfazed by her inability to utter a coherent sentence. "Ah ben a-hangin' around outside the Curtis Mercantile Store just a-hopin' to ketch a glimpse a' yore purty face—"

"No, no, no!" Rita threw up her hands and stepped between them. "Jack, whatever is your problem? You sound like you've got a mouthful of mush."

Bud drew back, his face a picture of astonishment. "I'm puttin' on a Texas accent. Thought that's what you wanted."

Rita stared at Bud while Kit covered her mouth with her hands to keep from laughing out loud. Finally Rita sighed. "Bud-Jack, talk natural."

"But—"

"Bud-Jack, trust me. You don't have to put on a Texas accent. Just talk natural."

Bud gave a skeptical grunt. "You're the boss. But I still think—"

"Talk *natural*, Bud-Jack."

"Natural. Okay, but I been to Chicago. Don't blame me if folks don't know I'm supposed to be a Texan." He drew a deep breath and began again. "Howdy, Miz Rose. Can I carry your packages for you?"

"That's mighty neighborly of you, Sheriff Jack." Kit jumped quickly back into character, slipping an imaginary basket from her arm and offering it to him.

Bud looked confused, then muttered, "Oh, yeah," and pretended to accept the basket that wasn't there. "Uh, say, Miz Rose, I was wonderin' if you'd care to go to the barn dance with me tomorrow night."

Kit batted her lashes at him. "I'd be honored to attend the dance with a fine upstanding gentleman such as yourself," she cooed.

Bud's grin grew wider. "Yeah, I am, ain't I?" He chuckled. "Well, Miz Rose, since I'm on kind of a roll here—" with exaggerated motions, he set aside the imaginary basket and straightened "—I got one more question for you."

"And what might that be, Sheriff?" Flutter-flutter went the eyelashes.

"Gotta getcha in the mood first," he declared—and lunged at her.

ACROSS THE ROOM, Boone tried to pay attention to the two men facing off against each other. Harry Meeks, a middle-aged mama's boy, bared his teeth in a grimace and jumped forward with both hands held aloft, elbows bent at ninety-degree angles, shouting, "Aha!"

Lee just stood there, a you've-got-to-be-kidding expression on his face. "Boone," he appealed to the man in charge, "do somethin', will ya?"

Harry straightened, looking pained. "I thought I did that rather well," he said primly.

Boone sighed and considered his "fighters." Lee was okay, but he'd have to speak to Rita about the very real probability that Harry was going to get his plow cleaned during the big fight unless they matched him up with some ninety-year-old grandma.

And what about the scene where Kit, as Rose, was to march into the saloon and give Harry-as-the-gunman a slap? Knowing Kit and the way she threw herself into everything she did, he figured she'd probably break the guy's jaw—knock out a handful of teeth at the very least.

Which wasn't such a bad idea, considering the way Harry had been giving her the eye. Boone knew men, being one himself, and he'd be willing to swear an oath that old Harry had a crush on her. He damn well better watch his step in the love scenes or—

It's none of your business, Boone reminded himself. Too bad he hadn't stuck to his guns about getting mixed up with Showdown Days, but this was the extent of his participation. Kit was a big girl now, and he wasn't about to get involved....

And he glanced toward the trio on the stage just in time to see that damned Bud Williams haul Kit into his arms.

KIT FELT as if she was being suffocated. And Bud's arms crushing the air from her beleaguered lungs wasn't even the worst of it, she realized as his lips descended toward hers.

"Sheriff Jack, have you lost your *mind?*" She struggled mightily. He retaliated by lifting her completely off the floor.

"Miz Rose, I love you! Will you be mine?" He panted in her ear, hanging on to her struggling form by brute strength. "Damn it, you know you're gonna, so lemme kiss you!"

It was no use; she wasn't strong enough to escape his iron grip. Why didn't somebody *do* something? If she could just get enough air in her lungs to scream—

Bud let go of her so suddenly that she stumbled backward and bumped into Rita. Catching her balance, Kit whirled around, fighting mad. She'd give Bud Williams a piece of her mind!

And then she saw Boone with a grip on her would-be suitor, a grip every bit as decisive as the one Bud had had on her. One of Boone's hands tangled in Bud's collar, which perhaps had something to do with the scarlet hue of that gentleman's cheeks. Boone's other hand tightened into a fist, cocked and ready for action.

"What's the matter with you people?" Rita's outraged shout brought everyone to attention. "Boone Taggart, you let go of my Sheriff Jack!"

"But Rita, he was—"

"I said, let him go! He may not be much, but he's all I've got."

Somewhat sheepishly, Boone let his fist fall to his side. He seemed to have more trouble uncurling his fingers from Bud's collar, but that, too, was eventually accomplished.

"And you, Bud Williams! What do you mean, jumping on my Miss Rose like a duck on a june bug? Shame on you!"

"But, Rita!" Bud swallowed hard and eased one finger inside his collar as if to loosen it. "I thought about it and I thought about it, and it seems to me Sheriff Jack would have kissed her before he just come out and bald-faced proposed matrimony. I just *felt* it was right."

Rita's jaw dropped. "I don't believe it. I've got a method actor here."

Bud jerked up, casting a self-righteous glance at Boone. "Yeah, that's it, all right. I definitely got a method."

They've all gone crazy, Kit decided, glaring at the three of them. "Now wait a minute! Don't I have anything to say about this?"

They turned expectantly toward her.

"Bud Williams, if you lay another hand on me before Showdown Days starts, I—I'll cut it off! You hear?"

Bud assumed an injured air. "Well, hell, Kit, what're you so bent outta shape about? I was only actin'."

"I'll take that for agreement," she said coldly, turning her ire on Rita. "And you—you're the one in charge! Were you just going to stand there and let him maul me?"

Rita threw up her hands in defeat. "Good grief, he wasn't showing much finesse, I'll grant you that, but he was hardly *mauling* you. However, your point's well taken and I apologize. Now can we *please* get on with rehearsal?"

Kit gave her head a violent shake. "Not so fast. I've got one more thing to say."

Bud snorted and backed away. "Well I don't want to hear it," he declared. "I'm gonna go get me a bottle of pop. Holler when we're ready to get some work done."

Kit ignored him and looked at Boone. He met her glance warily, and she could see him brace himself for the worst.

But this wasn't it. "Thanks," she said, her voice coming out small and contrite.

"Huh?" He looked astonished.

"I said thanks. For saving me, I mean. From a fate worse than death—literally." She gave a nervous little laugh. "Bud's not a bad guy—he just isn't into subtleties. I'm glad you were around."

"Me, too." But he frowned. "Think you'll have any more trouble with him?"

"No."

Rita's vehement "Yes!" seemed to surprise Boone as much as it did Kit.

"Well, I do," Rita insisted. "Maybe he won't be quite so eager to get his hands on my leading lady—"

"He damned well better not." Boone's lips drew back over his teeth.

"—but he's just not hero material. Furthermore, he's going to overpower everybody, especially..." She glanced guiltily toward Harry, who sat in a far corner of the room, calmly reading a large hardcover book.

Boone nodded. "Yeah, I meant to speak to you about Harry. I don't think the man's ever seen a punch thrown in anger. How the hell did he end up the villain of this piece?"

"Process of elimination."

Kit knew where Rita was heading. "Don't you think we should get back to work?" she suggested to change the subject.

"Not until I give Boone one more chance to bail us— the whole town—out of this predicament. Boone—"

"No."

"Boone—"

"No, thanks."

"Boone!"

"No, *damn it!*"

Kit listened to the exchange with mixed emotions. She didn't anticipate any further trouble with Bud, but the mere thought of playing opposite Boone in any capacity—either hero or villain—sent tingles of excitement racing up her backbone.

If it had been Boone pulling her into his arms a few minutes ago, she wouldn't have struggled at all.

"I won't ask again!" Rita concluded the conversation with Boone.

"Promises, promises," he called after her, his tone mocking.

But his expression said something else. Looking at him, Kit wondered if perhaps somewhere deep down Boone regretted having made such a strong stand against Showdown Days. Now he was stuck with it, and the Taggarts weren't the kind of men who enjoyed admitting they'd been wrong.

Rita clapped her hands for attention. "All right, people, let's try the scene where Rose goes into the saloon and slaps the gunfighter's face for punching out her brother. Kit, Harry, over here, please."

Kit glanced at Boone. "I have to go," she said breathlessly. "Th-thank you again."

He shifted from one foot to the other. "As I recall this scene, after you slap him he grabs you and kisses you, right?"

"That's right."

Boone frowned. "Want some advice?"

"About the kiss or the slap?"

"The slap. I'm pretty sure you can handle Harry in a clinch."

"Okay. I guess I could use some advice, since I've never slapped anyone in my entire life—or been slapped, for that matter."

Boone nodded with all seriousness. "Okay, here it is. I've been working with old Harry, so you don't have to worry. Just rare back and let 'er fly. He'll know what to do."

"You mean..." Kit frowned. "Shouldn't I pull my punch or... or something?"

"Nah. Pull your punch and you'll end up hurting the guy. And just to make it easier for you, I'll make myself scarce. Meet me in the drugstore after rehearsal, okay?"

Whistling a snappy tune, Boone walked out of the rehearsal hall.

"I DON'T KNOW what I did wrong. I honestly don't know what I did wrong."

Kit walked beside Boone toward the car parked several blocks away. She'd just pulled him out of the drugstore, where he'd been perusing magazines, into the street where she could tell her tale without fear of interruption.

She wrung her hands as she walked along. "I mean, I went roaring in there just like I was supposed to, demanding to know where that 'low-down polecat who beat up my brother' was. Harry—I mean Boone, the Mysterious Gunfighter—turns around from what's supposed to be the bar and says, 'Ma'am, you lookin' for me?' in his best Southern gentleman style."

"Who makes this stuff up?" Boone wondered out loud, taking her elbow to escort her across Stagecoach Street. "Do you think this production bears even the faintest resemblance to anything that ever actually happened?"

"Boone!" She whirled to pound a fist against his shoulder, venting at least a little of her frustration. "That's not the point! The point is, when he said that, I just hauled off and *whap!* Right across the face!"

"Now that sounds firmly rooted in probability," he said. "I'll bet it's what really—"

"I think I may have dislocated his jaw! When I tried to check for damage, he ran backward to get away from me, tripped over his own feet and fell flat. Boone, he hit his head on the floor and went out like a light! Fortunately Doc Preston walked in at that very moment—I don't know what Harry might have done if he'd come to and seen me bending over him. Boone, I think I gave him a concussion!"

"You hit Doc Preston, too?"

"Of course not, I hit Harry!"

"Again?"

"Once was enough!" Hysterical laughter bubbled in her throat and, to her horror, spilled over. "I assaulted the poor man! Harry's mother will never forgive me. If he refuses to come back to rehearsals, Rita will never forgive me! I'll never forgive me, either. I'm not Rose Taggart, I'm a menace! Oh, Boone, oh, Boone! It was the funniest thing... you ever..."

He stopped beneath a streetlight and turned to face her, grinning. "I know," he said. "I was watching through the window."

Nothing had ever felt as right as his arms gathering her close. She laughed until tears ran down her cheeks, and Boone laughed with her. When her near hysteria began to taper off, she found herself clinging weakly to him, her hands on his shoulders.

She had to get hold of herself. It would never do to spin more fantasies about this man who obviously found her eminently resistible. Oh, he might steal a kiss or two, but it didn't mean anything—to him, anyway. He didn't go for unsophisticated country girls; he went for sophisticated city women.

She swallowed hard and gave a last little gasp of laughter. "Why did you do it?" she asked, her voice muffled against his chest.

"Do what?"

"Trick me into slugging poor Harry."

"He may be 'poor Harry' but he's still a man. I took care of Bud for you, but you've also got a love scene to play with Harry. He's been eyeing you. I wanted you to have the upper hand in all future dealings with him."

She threw back her head so she could see Boone's face. Only, with the streetlight behind him, she couldn't see his expression. She frowned. "You mean to tell me you think Harry might give me—give any woman—trouble?"

"Sweetheart," he said, his voice suddenly low and intimate, "Harry's a man, and there's not a one of us you can trust."

"Don't be silly. I trust—"

He proved her wrong with a kiss. *Who's silly now?* she wondered dreamily, rising on tiptoe to slide her arms fully around his neck. *Oh, Boone, I love you so—*

Her eyes, which had drifted closed, snapped open. Pressing her hands against his shoulders, she gave him a shove. "Stop!" she cried the moment her lips were free of his.

"You're going to hit me, too?" he murmured, his mouth warm against her throat. "I may have created a monster."

She couldn't catch her breath; her lungs felt starved for oxygen. Her knees trembled, on the verge of buckling entirely, and she found herself clinging to him while he trailed kisses along the tender line of her jaw. "W-why are you doing this?" she gasped.

"Damned if I know. Maybe just to show you I'm human, too, no better than Bud or even good old Harry."

He had that all wrong. He might be human, but what he did to her had nothing in common with the way Bud or good old Harry or other men made her feel. In actual fact, he was probably ruining her for other men as long as she lived. She ought to tell him so, tell him to leave her alone....

"Want me to stop?" He pressed one hand against the small of her back, and before she could answer, kissed her again.

This time when she came up for air, she forced herself to do what she knew she must. "Yes," she gasped, "I do want you to stop."

He let her go without the slightest argument, and she was gratified and offended at the same time. But she'd done the right thing, she assured herself as they walked to the car. She knew she had.

All the way back to the ranch, Kit sat beside Boone trying to puzzle out what was happening between them. Tonight he had seemed almost...jealous—jealous of Bud, even of Harry. But that didn't make sense. Boone had no interest in her.

Did he?

Stealing a glance at him as they drove through the moonlight, she felt a tiny leap of hope. Maybe he did find her...interesting. Attractive, even. Whatever a man looked for in a woman...

Maybe if they could spend more time together, get past their differences, they might find some common ground.

"We're home," he said.

"Oh! I was a million miles away."

"I know." He released his seat belt and twisted toward her. "Kit, I think we need to talk."

"A-about what?"

"You. Me. Us. Thom T. Showdown. Showdown Days. The legend."

She laughed nervously. "The meaning of life?" she teased.

"Yeah, if we get around to it, why not? It's just that—"

"Dad-burn it, I'm talking to yawl!"

Thom T. yanked them out of their private world and into his by the force of the crutch he banged against the bumper. He hopped around the front of the car, barely hampered by his leg cast.

"What the hell?" Boone threw open the car door and jumped out. "What's your problem, you old reprobate?"

"I ain't got no problem, now that I've made up my mind," Thom T. yelled back, "now that I've decided to get the hell out of Dodge!"

CHAPTER EIGHT

THOM T. HOPPED around the room with the aid of one crutch, flailing the air with his free arm. Now that he'd made up his mind, it was obvious he saw no reason to tarry.

Kit clutched desperately at straws. "But shouldn't you think about it a little longer?"

"No, but somebody was bound to ask," the old cattleman complained. "Blood's thicker than water, Kitty. If Boone's convinced..." For a moment Thom T. looked every year of his age. "What I'm gonna do is go East to see my great-grandson. Everything else can wait 'till I get back. That satisfy you?"

It didn't, but she nodded numbly, anyway. Boone had won. She glanced at him through the lowered fringe of her lashes, dreading the triumph she would surely see on his face.

Considering that everything was going his way, Boone looked something less than victorious. Did he still think Thom T. might change his mind? Kit wondered hopefully.

"I wouldn't want you to sign anything until you're absolutely sure," Boone told his grandfather.

That old gentleman gave a most ungentlemanly snort. "Never you fear that, sonny-boy." He turned toward the door, leaning heavily on his crutch. "I've said my piece,

and I'm runnin' down faster than a two-dollar watch. I'll
see you young folks in th' mornin'."

Both Boone and Kit started forward. "I'll give you a
hand, Grandpa.... Let me—"

"I ain't helpless!" Thom T. braced the crutch beneath
his arm and swung up the tip, as if to hold them off. "I
said in the mornin'!"

Kit watched him stamp out of sight, thinking, *So that's
that. It's over. The Rocking T will pass out of Taggart
hands. An era is ending.*

What could she say? Shoulders drooping, she turned to
leave. A hand on her arm stopped her, but she couldn't
face Boone, so she just stood there, stiff and unhappy.

"Kit, it's for the best."

"Is it?"

"If you think about it logically, you'll know it is. He's
old. He needs family."

"Everybody needs family, even you. You're thinking of
yourself, not him. You've lost sight of what this is all
about—the uprooting of an old man whose heart and soul
will always be here no matter where you take him. Some
things you just can't change."

She swung around then, unable to maintain even a fa-
cade of stoicism. Past a haze of misery, she saw his
smooth expression—the lawyer face she hated. Anger
whipped through her, and she yanked her arm from his
light grip.

"I guess you always get what you want, but this time
you're wrong," she blazed. "Thom T...Thom T.'s like a
wild mustang—civilization will kill him! But you won and
the consequences are on your head. There's nothing I can
do about it."

She should leave now, but somehow she couldn't. *Say
it,* she commanded herself. *Say it all. Burn those bridges.*

You have nothing left to hope for, nothing left to dream about. Finish it here and now.

He said her name, his voice husky, but she ignored the appeal she heard there and plunged on.

"Nothing I can do about it except promise you that I will *never* forgive you."

"You don't mean that, Kitty."

"I do. Oh, I do!"

"Daniel Boone Taggart, the man who has everything." His sister-in-law, Meg, had said that not so long ago. Now Kit was telling him, "I guess you always get what you want."

Same song, different verse, from the two women whose opinions he valued most. Watching Kit walk away with her head high and her small hands clenched into fists at her sides, Boone wondered if he hadn't lost by winning.

He had everything and nothing; he got what he wanted and was no longer sure he wanted it. He shook his head fiercely, wondering when he had begun to doubt himself.

Damn it, he *was* right about this. His grandfather could be happy in the East; all it took was being surrounded by the right people. Now only one question remained:

Without the right people, can I be happy in the East?

Boone tried several times to speak privately to Kit the next day, but each time she managed to avoid him. She'd spent a sleepless night and her eyes and head ached; she was in no mood to listen to sugarcoated explanations.

She did make a point of talking to Thom T., though — for all the good it did.

"I know what I'm doin', girl," the old man said gruffly. "Don't you start on me now."

"I won't start on you," she vowed in a ragged voice. "I just want you to be happy. I guess you're old enough to figure out what'll do that without any help from me."

"Naw, that ain't it. We just done enough jawbonin' about it, is all."

His glance seemed furtive somehow, and she couldn't imagine why. Not that it mattered. She gave him an uncertain smile. "You're right, so let's change the subject. When will you and Boone be heading to Boston?"

"Soon's we can—tomorrow, most likely."

"Okay. While you're gone I'll move into town."

She waited for his protest. And waited. Until finally she realized that no protest was forthcoming. Her lips parted in sorrow and disbelief.

He nodded sheepishly. "That's prob'ly for the best," he admitted. "It'd prob'ly be best regardless of my comin's and goin's"

"Y-you...you don't want me here anymore?" She felt as if he'd just driven another nail into her coffin.

"It ain't that. It's just—dad-gum it, gal, I ain't gonna last forever, even if I stay in Texas. You shouldn't be stuck way out here with an old goat like me. You should be livin' in town, lettin' the young bucks squire you around. You need a husband—you should be babysittin' a houseful of kids, not an old stove-up cowboy in his second childhood."

And that was that; her presence here was only making matters worse for Thom T. She hadn't thought it possible to feel any lower, but she'd been wrong.

Boone was busy all day with arrangements and details of the trip, and Kit was busy with rehearsals. The two men would leave the following day; if she could just stay out of Boone's path until then...

She almost made it—almost. In the car ready to leave for the airport, Thom T. rolled down his window, air-conditioning be damned.

"Found a place yet?" he asked Kit.

She kept her attention centered on him, although she realized that Boone, in the act of entering the car, had turned to look at her. "Not yet. But don't worry, I'll be gone before you get back."

"Gone where?" Boone asked.

"I ain't worried," Thom T. denied, ignoring his grandson's question. "I mean I am, but not about that. I'm worried about you findin' a suitable place, so I found one for you. Miz Baker's got a nice apartment over her garage. She says you can—"

"Thom T., let me do this on my own, okay? I'm certainly capable of finding—"

"What in the hell are you two talking about?" Boone leaned forward, one arm draped across the roof of the car, jaw thrust out and an angry light in his eyes.

Kit's ire rose to meet his. "I'm moving into town—what did you expect? When Thom T. sells the ranch, I don't go with it like another barn or corral!"

He looked furious enough to vault over the top of the car to shake some sense into her. Then as abruptly as if someone had pushed a switch, the fire disappeared and the lawyer mask descended. When he spoke, not so much as a trace of Texas tinged his voice.

"No, of course not, but there's no special hurry. Take your time and find what you really want, then send the particulars to me and I'll take care of everything."

"W-what are you talking about?"

He raised his brows, his expression cool. "I mean I'll take care of everything," he repeated with exaggerated patience. "We're not sending you away homeless, *Katherine*."

Kit had never felt so insulted in her life. "I don't need your charity!" she cried. "As you so recently pointed out, I'm not a Taggart, so you don't owe me a blasted thing!"

"Suit yourself." He shrugged. "But don't make a hasty decision you'll regret."

Thom T. reached through the open window to pat her hand. "He means, don't cut off your nose to spite your face. That's good advice, gal. Don't let him get you so riled you—"

"Thom T., I love you dearly, but if I never see that turncoat grandson of yours again, it'll be too soon!"

She whirled and ran for the house. She felt the broiling Texas sun on her back, felt tears streaking down her cheeks, heard the pounding of her feet in time with the tempo of her heartbeat. But what she most longed for, she neither felt nor heard—Boone's hand on her shoulder, his footsteps behind her, his voice calling out to her.

All she heard was the sound of the car as it pulled slowly out of the ranch yard.

She'd have felt better if he'd peeled rubber.

"WHAT IN THE WORLD is the matter with you?" Rita sounded exasperated. "You look like you haven't slept in a week."

Kit groaned. She knew how she looked; she'd seen the dark circles under her eyes and the haunted expression on her face. She'd hoped Rita would have been too polite to mention it. "Don't worry, I'll get my act together in time for Showdown Days," she said—and burst into tears.

Rita dropped her omnipresent clipboard and took the younger woman in her arms, uttering comforting phrases liberally laced with "there-theres." After a few minutes,

Kit swallowed hard and drew back. Rita pulled a small packet of tissues from the pocket of her skirt and offered it.

Kit mopped her eyes. "I'm sorry," she apologized. "It's just that Boone and Thom T...." She was unable to continue.

"I heard they'd gone East for a visit," Rita said gently.

"Yes, but did you hear that Thom T.'s going to sell the ranch and move there permanently?"

Rita paled. "You're kidding!"

"I wish." Miserably Kit rolled the sodden tissue between her fingers. "This is all Boone's doing. If I could get my hands on him I'd just...!" She gritted her teeth.

Rita sat down on a folding wooden chair. "I can hardly believe this," she murmured. "Showdown without the Taggarts—impossible to imagine."

Kit nodded and sniffed harder.

"Thom T.'s done so much for so many of us." Rita sounded shaken.

"You, too?" Kit knew Thom T. had a special fondness for Rita and her family, but had never known why.

"He gave Joe the money to start the lumberyard. *Gave* it, Kit. He said the Taggarts owed the Lopezes more than that for all they'd done for the Rocking T over the years." Rita shook her dark head wonderingly. "Joe didn't even know it, but one of his ancestors was *segundo*—trail boss—on Rocking T cattle drives back in the 1870s."

"That's just like Thom T.," Kit said. "I'll bet there's not a family in town he hasn't helped in one way or another. Without the Taggarts, there probably wouldn't even *be* a town. Drat that Boone!"

Rita looked surprised. "Why do you always blame Boone? Thom T.'s got a mind of his own."

"Because Boone found the buyer for the ranch and talked Thom T. into selling. He's the one who wants to drag Thom T. back East to live. You know what I think? I think it's a guilty conscience, that's what I think! Boone's been a rotten grandson, and now he thinks he can waltz in here and...and... Why are you shaking your head?"

"Because Boone's not like that."

Kit frowned. "How can you be so sure?"

"Because I've known Boone Taggart all his life, and he's not like that," Rita repeated stubbornly. "Whatever he's doing, he truly believes it's the best thing for his grandfather. And if he decides he's wrong, he'll admit it."

Rita stood up and put a comforting arm around Kit's shoulders, squeezing lightly. "Honey, I know you're hurtin', but cut Boone some slack, okay? I saw the two of you together—"

Kit recoiled. "What's that supposed to mean?"

"You're too mad right now to listen if I told you." Rita glanced down at her wristwatch. "Besides, we're late for rehearsal. Best thing you can do is put your mind on something else for a while. Pretending to be in love with Bud Williams should distract you from reality!"

"Miz Rose, you dance divinely."

"Uh, Harry, I don't think a vicious frontier gunman would use the word 'divine' in any form."

"Oh. Perhaps you're right. Okay, how about this? Miz Rose, you dance with spritely grace. Better?"

"Jack, I'm so frightened! That horrible gunman's brought his whole gang to town. What if he tries to stop our wedding?"

"Now, now, don't you worry your purty little head none, Rosie. If them desperadoes want hot lead at high noon, they come to the right place. Or cold steel for breakfast—hell, it's all the same to me. I'll take 'em on one at a time or by the bunch. I'll mop up Main Street with 'em! By damn, I'll make 'em sorry they ever— Whattaya mean I'm overdoin' it? I laid awake all night thinkin' up that speech!"

"THESE FEATHERS look stupid! Look at 'em droop over my eyes. I'm not gonna wear 'em!"

"Wear the feathers, Sissy. Wear the blasted feathers, or it's goodbye, dance-hall girl, hello, quilting bee!"

"Okay, okay, you don't have to get tacky about it...."

" ... AND SHE READ about it in some newspaper in California? No kiddin'?"

"Yeah, and some big magazine was here takin' pictures just the other day. Boy, howdy—looks like we'll have folks comin' from shore to shore and border to border."

"Showdown Days is goin' big time, yes-siree-bob!"

" ... SORRY DWAYNE, I thought you were Shayne. I don't care what your girlfriend says, members of the outlaw gang have to grow whiskers—or at least serious stubble. You can tell her I said so...."

"WHAT'S THE MATTER, Kit?"

Kit, seated on the stone steps of the little church on the hill at one end of Main Street, glanced around to see Doc Preston watching her with a quizzical expression on his round pleasant face.

He lowered himself beside her. "You're lookin' a little down at the mouth, missy. Must be lonesome out at the ranch with Boone and Thom T. away."

"I'm not living there anymore. I've moved into the apartment over Mrs. Baker's garage."

"Oh?" Doc's brows rose. Apparently deciding her living arrangements were none of his business, he made another stab at conversation. "I bet you're beginning to think we'll never be able to pull this show off. Am I right?"

Kit smiled ruefully. "It'd take a miracle."

"We get that miracle every year, regular as clockwork."

"But this isn't like every other year," she pointed out. "This year Bud's got the bit between his teeth and is acting more like a bully than a Noble Sheriff. Harry is about as believable as a Mysterious Gunman as I am as a... as a..."

Doc's eyes twinkled. "As a dance-hall girl?"

"Thanks." She gave him a woeful glance. "Have you seen Harry leading his alleged gang? Dub Partridge could break him in two with one hand, and the twins keep playing practical jokes on the poor man—Shayne put molasses in his hat and Dwayne stuck a burr under his saddle and the horse ran away with him. I don't know how much more Harry can take, especially since he didn't want to be here in the first place."

Doc pulled a pipe from the pocket of his shirt. "It'll all work out," he said serenely, tapping the bowl against the side of the steps. He flashed her an amused look. "I say this every year, you know. People somehow rise to the occasion."

Kit took small comfort from his words as the afternoon dragged on—less, watching Harry-the-gunman trying to punch out Rose's brother, James. Lee Cox did his best as James, but it had long since become clear that what Harry knew about throwing a punch could be inscribed on the head of a pin, with room left over for The Lord's Prayer.

Finally Lee gave up and took a solo pratfall. Rita flung down her clipboard in disgust while Kit, muffling anxious laughter, walked away shaking her head. Things were going from bad to worse. Nerves stretched ever tighter as Showdown Days drew inexorably closer.

Distracted, Kit wandered into the small graveyard behind the whitewashed church and found herself staring at the neatly fenced headstone of a burial plot.

"Here lies the man called Boone. Lived by the gun and died likewise. RIP 1876."

Succinct and to the point, the headstone marked the final resting place of the man who started all this. Kit knelt beside the small marker, realizing that one Boone or another was at the heart of all her troubles.

This Boone had died like a yellow dog in the streets; everyone in Showdown knew that. But he had apparently cared enough about Miss Rose to put up a fight for her. It hadn't been a fair fight. Only the iron nerves and fast gun of Sheriff Jack had stood between this desperado and his evil heart's desire, but at least this Boone had fought for what he wanted.

"Who makes this stuff up?" Boone Taggart had sounded incredulous when he'd asked that question. The answer was, of course, that no one made it up. The legend was true; it had to be. The town couldn't be built upon a lie. More than anything, she wanted to believe that right made might, that truth and justice would triumph. But did they always?

The *truth* was, she loved Boone Taggart—always had and always would. If there was any *justice* in this world, he'd return her love.

She gave a bitter little laugh at her own whimsy and stood. The time for spinning daydreams and living on false hope was long past. She'd had a letter from Thom T. just yesterday, telling her in his fine spidery penmanship that he'd seen a "nice little spread" in Connecticut with a farmhouse dating back to Revolutionary days—revolution in any form appealed to the old man.

"Of course, the whole state of Connecticut would fit into one little bitty corner of the King Ranch," he wrote, "but it ain't like I'm fixing to run cows."

She supposed it was settled, then. If Thom T. was happy, then she must be happy, too. And she would be— she would.

Someday.

"Kit! Kit, where are you?"

At Rita's call, Kit started toward the front of the church. Enough of this self-pity, she told herself firmly. Showdown Days were almost here and she was going to be the best Rose Taggart there ever was—excluding the real one, of course.

She should look at the bright side; at least Boone wouldn't be around to make her even more nervous.

"HARRY, YOU *CAN'T* QUIT. You can't *do* this to us!"

"I can. I have!"

Rounding the corner in response to the summons, Kit heard the fire in Harry Meeks's voice. Why, that was the way Boone, the Mysterious Gunman, should talk! For a moment, his meaning failed to register, so impressed was she with his delivery.

Rita and Harry stood in the center of an awed circle of onlookers—extras, mainly, and various behind-the-scenes workers. All stared at the trembling man in the black hat.

The wet black hat. And the wet black shirt and trousers and boots.

"B-but I don't understand." Rita's usually composed features were tight.

"Then I'll tell you!" Harry swung around, including each and every one of them within the scope of his scorn. His enraged attention settled on Kit, and he lifted one trembling hand to point a bony finger.

"You! It began with you! You gave me a concussion!"

"But I apologized." Everybody was looking at her. She almost wished she were beneath the headstone with Boone, the Mysterious Gunman.

"Fat lot of good that did. You made a fool of me, and I've been the butt of jokes ever since." Harry ripped the wet black hat from his head and flung it onto the ground. "I'm mad as hell and I'm not going to take this anymore!"

"Yes, Harry, yes!" Rita grabbed his arm and he winced. "That's the kind of macho magnetism we need in this part. You've got it, Harry. You've really got it!"

"I do?" His pointing finger wavered and dropped; he frowned. Suddenly seeming to realize he was about to be victimized yet again, he uttered an exasperated, "Oh, no, you don't!" and fixed Rita with a gimlet eye. "Don't try to jolly me out of it. My mind is made up. When my so-called gang dumped me in the horse trough, it was the last straw."

"We only done that because we like you," wheedled Shayne Partridge.

His identical burly brother, Dwayne, nodded. "Hell, yes! And all them other thangs, too—the burr and the molasses and the motor oil—"

"The motor oil!" Rita's face blanched.

Dwayne shifted on his big booted feet. "Yeah, well, that 'un didn't work, so let's don't talk about it. I shouldn't even a' brung it up."

"Don't quit, Harry," Shayne chimed in. "You do, and word gets back to our pa that it's our fault, and he's gonna whup our—"

"Save your breath!" Harry fumbled for the buckle to his gunbelt, then finally found it. The six-shooters dropped around his boots. His sparse blond hair looked even paler in contrast to a face gone beet red. "I did this only as a favor to you, Rita—you, a teacher and all. I saw you striving to bring a modicum of erudition and culture to this . . . this sorry excuse for a town. But—"

"And you were right, Harry, right! Don't desert me in my hour of need—we can work this out," Rita beseeched. "You can't quit. People come hundreds, thousands of miles even, just for Showdown Days. And you're the star, Harry! Without you, we have no show."

Harry shrugged.

Rita repeated with more emphasis, "We have no show without you! Please, for the good of the entire town, for the good of untold generations of Showdownians living, dead and yet to be born, I beg you—"

Harry held up his hands. With his pistols at his feet and his hat on the ground, he seemed to have regained most of his composure. "My decision," he said, "is immutable. Let one of these—" he flung an arm toward the Partridge brothers "—gentlemen—" his lip curled "—take up the gauntlet and pull the town's collective chestnuts from the fire! Because you don't have Harry Meeks to kick around any more!"

THE EMERGENCY MEETING that night at the Yellow Rose Saloon drew practically the entire population of Showdown—with the exception of Harry Meeks and his mother, who had already left for an extended vacation in Wichita Falls. It was a subdued and unhappy group who faced Rita and Kit.

In sonorous tones, the townspeople one by one laid out the full extent of the economic damage the town would suffer if the Showdown Days pageant folded at this late date—disaster not only this year but forever after, because all credibility would be destroyed.

Finally Doc Preston rose, pipe in hand. The unhappy buzz of conversation died away in deference to the popular physician, who waited for complete silence before speaking.

"I'm surprised at all of you," he scolded, "ready to throw in the towel. Showdown Days isn't in trouble. All we need to do is replace one actor. It's an inconvenience, nothing more. Whoever takes the part will only have a couple of days to get up on it, but so what? It's not like we don't all know the story."

A chorus of groans and catcalls greeted this pronouncement, but Doc continued undiminished. "It's not that big a deal," he insisted. "Shoot, I could do it myself in a pinch."

"No offense, Doc, but when's the last time you was on a horse?" Dub Partridge called out.

Doc laughed along with the rest of them. "Point well taken, Dub. I said I *could*. I didn't say it'd be *necessary*."

"Then who's gonna do it?" Sissy Williams demanded. "Unless you can snag somebody out of thin air, I don't see. . . ."

Her gaze followed Doc's and her voice trailed away. Kit, watching Sissy, saw her eyes go wide and excitement transform her face.

"You don't mean . . . ?"

"Yes, Sissy, I do." Doc's broad grin included them all. "Ladies and gentlemen, may I suggest to you that the man born to play the part of Boone, the Mysterious Gunman, is right here in our midst. And ladies and gentlemen, his name is . . ." He pointed dramatically.

"Boone Taggart!"

CHAPTER NINE

WHAT WAS BOONE DOING HERE? Kit's mouth went dry. He was supposed to be back East. Had he come back to gloat over the Showdown Days debacle?

Ah, but he did look wonderful, leaning against the rear wall, his booted feet crossed at the ankles. He wore denim and an old black Stetson perched atop his dark hair—his shaggy dark hair, she realized with surprise. His slight smile made him look relaxed and . . . insolent, she decided. Like the Boone she remembered.

Like the Boone she first fell in love with.

A collective groan rocked the room in response to Doc's declaration. There couldn't be a person present who didn't know that Boone had adamantly refused to have anything to do with Showdown Days.

Rita gave the doctor an injured look. "That's plain tacky of you, Doc, getting our hopes up that way," she said. "I've already offered Boone the part of the gunslinger, or any other part he might want. Hell, I'd let him play Rose if he wanted to take a whack at it."

The crowd gasped; teachers weren't supposed to use swear words even in moments of great stress.

Doc looked neither offended by her language nor contrite. "Give it one more try," he suggested, his eyes twinkling. "I got a sneaking suspicion that we might prevail on Mr. Taggart to reconsider."

The room erupted, this time in excitement. Kit lost sight of Boone as townspeople descended upon him; when next the sea of bodies parted he was advancing on the stage, taking great strides with his long legs.

He vaulted up and stood beside the dumbfounded Rita. Grinning broadly, he held up his hands for quiet.

"Fellow Showdownians, looks like I'll have to bow to the greater good," he announced with appropriate modesty. "If you honestly think I'm the man for the job, I'll make you a deal—"

"Just a double-damned minute, here!" Bud's roar shocked the twittering audience into silence. Without further ado, he also bounded onto the stage.

He glowered at Boone. "If'n you think for one minute you can take over as Sheriff Jack, you got another think comin'. *I'm* Sheriff Jack and I *ain't* gonna play that damned gunfighter again this year. And that's that."

Bud crossed his arms over his chest and planted his boots wide, daring Boone or anyone else to take umbrage with his pronouncement.

Boone held up his hands to quiet the crowd. "Bud, old buddy, I wouldn't dream of messin' with your only chance to play the Hero," he said. "The only deal I'm interested in is this—I'll play the Mysterious Gunfighter and in return—"

Kit, sitting frozen in the front row, bolted to her feet. "In that case," she cried, "*I* quit!" Everyone had a limit and she'd reached hers. Performing with Boone Taggart? Being kissed by Boone Taggart in front of the whole world? She'd die first!

But before she could turn and run, Boone jumped lightly down beside her and caught her hands in his. "This'll work," he said, bending to look squarely into her face. "Trust me, Kitty."

Bedlam erupted around her, yet she heard his words with such clarity they might have been communicated telepathically. She shook her head wildly. "No! Isn't it enough you've ruined my life? Do you have to make a fool of me, too?"

He winced and his dark brows drew together. "Is that what you think I'm doing?" His hands tightened over hers.

"Yes!" She tried to pull free and failed. "Why did you come back? Haven't you hurt me enough?"

For a moment he simply looked at her. Then he sighed and raised his hands for silence.

"Any of you got any influence with the lady?" he asked a crowd threatening to turn surly. "Because unless she changes her mind, we still got a problem."

He jumped back up onto the stage. "While yawl are talkin' it over, I'll just have me a few words with our director."

He took Rita's arm and led her to the rear of the stage. Kit had just a glimpse of Rita's desperate expression before being surrounded by what seemed like the entire population of Showdown, all of them unanimously demanding that she straighten up and fly right.

Kit knew she didn't have a leg to stand on; she knew the second after she announced she was quitting that she wouldn't be able to make it stick. She'd reacted out of pure terror and wild desperation. The thought of rehearsing with Boone, appearing as Rose with him, made her nearly sick with apprehension.

It was too intimate. Scenes that with Harry were purely mechanical would take on new meaning with Boone—especially scenes in which he made advances toward her. The tension between them in real life might add realism to their performance, but at what cost?

And what about the other tension, that between Boone and Bud? Their two characters would have a number of close encounters of the physical kind; somebody could get hurt. Kit's stomach clenched with dread.

But she didn't say any of these things to the people shouting out all the reasons she couldn't quit on them now. In the end, she surrendered as she knew she must.

As Boone knew she must, judging from his slight smile when he received the news that Kit was back in the show. Rita, on the other hand, looked shaken to the core. She made a helpless little gesture, and Boone nodded and signaled for silence.

"I've just conferred with our director, and she'd like me to tell you that there will be a few changes in the scenario," Boone announced.

"The scen-what?" Bud demanded.

"The plot." Boone looked like the cat who'd swallowed the cream. "We're about to interject a dose of reality into the proceedings. It's time for a little revisionist history."

"But . . . but . . . hey, we don't have time. What're you talkin' about?"

Objections and questions swirled around him, and he waited for the tumult to die down before answering. "All changes will be on a need-to-know basis," he explained. "And most of you *don't* need to know—just play your parts as rehearsed. The only ones affected are Sheriff Jack and the outlaw gang. The rest of you can be excused."

Kit gave him an injured glance that asked silently, *What about me?* Boone flashed her a quick smile and a slight shake of his head before turning to lead Dwayne and Shayne to a quiet corner.

Kit waited for Rita at the stage steps. "What in the name of heaven's going on, Rita?" she demanded.

Rita looked in a state of shock. "He's got proof, Kit."

"Proof of what?"

"Proof that we've been doing it all wrong." Rita gave a helpless shrug. "I could hardly turn down a Taggart armed with proof, could I?"

"Why not?" Kit was seething. "Isn't this a rather late date to be making changes? Where'd this alleged proof come from, anyway?"

"From Thom T." Rita let out her breath in a groan. "My only consolation is we're so messed up this year that I don't think it'll make any difference. But even if it does, I promised him if he brought me proof I'd make changes. He did and now I've got to. I had no choice."

"I suppose." Kit's interest perked up. "So, tell me, what are these things we've been doing all wrong?"

But Rita just threw up her hands and referred all questions to Boone.

Kit sat and fumed while waiting for Boone's meeting with Bud and the three outlaws to end. It did—with a bang. Bud let out a roar that could surely be heard two blocks away.

"No! That ain't how it happened! Everybody knows...."

Boone said something much too low to catch, and Bud subsided, but when he walked past a few minutes later he was muttering under his breath and casting mutinous glances behind him.

The gang of Shayne, Dwayne and father went out the back way. Suddenly Kit realized that only she and Boone remained. She stood as he walked toward her, his smile cautious.

"Thanks for waiting," he said. "We've got a lot to talk a—"

"No, we don't." Kit cut him off ruthlessly, aware of danger in his unexpected about-face. The big-city lawyer was gone; the Texas cowboy was back. She didn't know what game he was playing, but she was having none of it.

He kept on smiling. "But—"

"I meant what I said. We're finished. We're not kin, we're not friends, and we're certainly not—" She bit her lip, halting the angry flow of words just in time.

But he knew and supplied the missing word. "Lovers?"

Kit straightened her shoulders, furious with herself for the heat she felt suffusing her cheeks. "I was going to say.... Oh, never mind what I was going to say. I waited because I want to know how Thom T. is—and where he is."

"Still back East, enjoying his great grandson and terrorizing the help."

"And you—when did you get here?"

"Day before yesterday."

"But...!" How could she not have heard? "No one told me," she finished lamely.

"You'd have known, if you hadn't moved into town."

Thank heaven she had! She could just imagine what it would be like living alone with him at the Rocking T. "Your comings and goings are of no further concern to me," she announced stiffly. "I'm simply interested in surviving Showdown Days. Now, what is this balderdash about changing the script?"

Again the Cheshire-cat smile. "We're about to correct history. It's on a need-to-know basis, and Rose doesn't need to know."

She regarded him with suspicion. "That doesn't make sense. This whole thing is *about* Rose. How will I know what to do?"

"Do what you've rehearsed. You won't have any problems if you follow your instincts. Trust me." Again the smile that made her knees buckle.

"I'd sooner trust a sidewinder," she declared. "Daniel Boone Taggart, if you mess this up . . . !"

"I know—you'll never forgive me. Which isn't much of a threat, considering that you're already never forgiving me for about eight other things."

He reached out to touch her chin, tilting it with his fingers. *I should pull away and march right out of here,* she told herself indignantly even while she continued to stare up into his fathomless blue-gray eyes.

With his thumb, he lightly traced the curve of her chin, sparking a wildfire that spread through her veins. "Kitty . . ." he murmured.

She couldn't let him kiss her! He was merely playing around with the local talent; she must protect herself. She had her self-respect to consider, whether he did or not.

With a little moan, she turned her face away. His mouth grazed her cheekbone and she shuddered. "Don't," she said thickly. "Please . . . don't."

"You don't mean that." He cupped her face between his hands and turned her gently to face him. "Don't you know why I've come back, Kit?"

"To prove a point, I suppose. Maybe to prove a lot of points." She stepped away, dragging a deep breath into her straining lungs. "To prove you *can* come back, even at the last minute, and be hailed as the conquering hero."

He frowned, cocking his head to one side. "You don't believe that."

He had never looked more attractive to her, or more accessible. She had to keep in mind it was all a pose.

She forced herself to meet his gaze without wavering. "That's exactly what I think. But you've proven other

things, as well—that you always get what you want, even
if you have to manipulate people into making disastrous
decisions they'll regret as long as they live.''

"Are you talking about Thom T.—or yourself?"

"Why..." She'd been talking about Thom T., but it
applied to herself as well, she realized belatedly. If she let
Boone manipulate her into a fling, she'd regret it for as
long as she lived. She took a step back. "Stay away from
me, Daniel Boone Taggart! I don't want anything to do
with you!"

"Kit, you don't—"

"If you tell me one more time that I don't mean what
I'm saying..." *Calm down, Kit. You're losing it.* "I'm
going through with Showdown Days because, well, because I *have* to for the good of the town. But I don't have
to like it, and once it's over I never have to see *you* again."

"Then I guess I've got my work cut out for me, changing your mind," he said, his tone level but slightly chal-
lenging. So much for her ultimatum. "That gives me a
week to do my damnedest."

"Don't even think about it!" She tossed her head and
glared at him. "The original Boone had a better chance
with Miss Rose than you do with me—and he got shot for
his troubles!"

Sunday, Day One

LOCAL RESIDENTS in costume cordoned off Main Street
early Sunday morning, marking the official beginning of
Showdown Days. At each end of the street they erected
wooden signs proclaiming the town to be Jones, Texas, in
the year 1876.

Most of the morning was spent ridding the street of evidence of the twentieth century. All motorized vehicles

were escorted from the area for the week of the celebration, and hitching rails for horses quickly installed.

By noon the street swarmed with kids, dogs, carriages and riders on horseback. While the men helped set up craft displays in shops and windows, women gathered in the parlor of the reconstructed Lone Star Hotel to begin the quilting bee. The resulting quilt would be raffled, a popular feature of the Friday-night barn dance.

Kit, ensconced in a room at the hotel for the duration, slept as late as she could and then lay there listening to the hustle and bustle outside. She knew she'd need all the rest she could get to prepare herself for the strain of being on almost constant public display for the week.

When she couldn't stand it any longer, she jumped out of bed. Trembling with a mixture of excitement and trepidation, she climbed into three petticoats, a blue-flowered gingham dress and high button shoes. Pulling her hair to the back of her head, she secured the unruly mass with a handful of pins.

Just a few days and this ordeal will be over, she promised her reflection in the mirror. Then Boone would go off to New York or London or Timbuktu and she'd never have to see him again.

The woman in the mirror stared back, pale and unhappy. For a moment Kit thought longingly of the powdered blusher inside her purse but decided against it. Instead, she pinched her cheeks lightly to give them some color. If she was going to play the part, she reminded herself as she descended to the lobby, she'd play it fair and square.

Once downstairs, she was so swept up by the excitement the day passed quickly. This first day, in fact, was mostly a shakedown period to allow everyone to get into

character; the legend would not begin to unfold until
Monday.

Which meant that Boone would not be seen today. That
fact alone was enough to relax Kit, once she grew accustomed to unfamiliar and unwieldy clothing, and to seeing her friends and neighbors likewise encumbered. She
even found it relatively easy to flirt with Sheriff Jack when
he sauntered past on the boardwalk in the person of Bud
Williams, readily pulling out his Colt revolvers to explain
to wide-eyed children—and not a few men—how they
worked.

By the time she lowered the wick on her kerosene lamp
Sunday night, she felt truly immersed in the part of Rose
Taggart. Even talking to tourists had been fun, although
she was well aware that today had been only a small sam-
pling of what was to come. More and more people would
stream into town until, by Saturday, when the classic
shoot-out on Main Street occurred, the area would be
clogged with onlookers.

Lying in bed, keyed up and sleepless, Kit tried to convince herself that the rest of the week would go as well as
today had. For the next six days, she was Rose Taggart,
not Kit McCrae. And Boone Taggart was really a low-
down gun-toting snake who would briefly make a pest of
himself, but in the end, meet his proper comeuppance.

Monday, Day Two

"HE'S COMIN' DOWN Main Street and he's ridin' that
black Outlaw horse!"

Rita's twelve-year-old son, Mike, leaned inside the
parlor door to shout the news, then just as quickly darted
away. Kit, plying a needle with the rest of the women,

started with surprise and managed to jab her finger painfully.

She didn't need to ask who *he* was.

Clutching scraps of calico in one hand, she hurried outside, the other quilters behind her. On the boardwalk she came to an abrupt stop, taken aback by the number of onlookers gathered there. All eyes were turned toward the west....

Dark horse, dark rider. At the sight of Boone atop the black devil that had injured Thom T., Kit caught her breath. The stallion sidestepped down Main Street, neck arched and eyes rolling. Boone held the animal on a tight rein and there could be no doubt who was in charge.

Kit noticed the most minute details of the horse: the flecks of foam on his muzzle as he chewed at the bit, the lather visible around the edges of the saddle blanket, the dark streaks of sweat on neck and flanks. Boone must have ridden him all the way from the Rocking T, she realized, probably to take the edge off the animal before exposing him to the crowds.

The pair came on, amid growing murmurs of appreciation. When she could procrastinate no longer, Kit slowly raised her gaze from horse to rider—and she, too, gasped.

Dressed all in black, Boone rode in dark solitude, looking neither right nor left. Stetson pulled low over his forehead, he might have been alone for all the notice he took of those around him. Twin Colt revolvers rested on his hips as if they belonged there, and he moved gracefully in the saddle.

Here was a hard dangerous man, and it was this sense of danger that excited the crowd. If they only knew that he was, in fact, a sophisticated international attorney!

Abreast of the boardwalk where Kit stood, Boone suddenly reined in the Outlaw. Kit—and everyone near her—

gasped and recoiled from this dark and threatening intruder. With laconic grace, he swung from the saddle and tossed the reins over the hitching post.

To Kit's surprise, the Outlaw didn't bolt but stood quivering. Perhaps Boone was the only person not surprised, for he didn't spare as much as a glance for the animal, instead, bounding up the steps to stand before Kit.

He swept the hat from his head with mock gallantry. His hard mouth twisted in a faintly menacing smile. "Ma'am," he said. "I expect you'd be Miss Rose Taggart."

His knowing glance traveled from her eyes to her mouth, and suddenly Kit realized she'd been soothing her pricked finger with her tongue. Hastily she jerked her hand away and thrust it behind her. "I—I'm Miss Taggart," she admitted, "but I'm not accustomed to addressing strangers on a public street."

With a toss of her head, she turned toward the hotel door, careful not to let her calico skirts brush his black boots in the process. She heard his voice behind her saying, "We won't be strangers for long, Miss Taggart. You may rely upon it."

Applause covered her exit.

Tuesday, Day Three

RIDERS AT THE FOOT of Main Street sawed at the reins, trying to settle their excited animals long enough for the starter to fire his pistol into the air and begin the race. Record throngs surged the length of the street, packed together on boardwalks and crowding balconies.

Kit, holding a small parasol over her right shoulder, took her place on the seat of a buckboard waiting near the finish line. When Sheriff Jack won, she had to be handy to give him a congratulatory kiss.

Thus far, Showdown Days had proceeded in style. Despite Rita's fears about lack of rehearsal time, despite Boone's insistence on doing things his own way, nothing of any significance had gone wrong. Even Bud had settled into his role as the sheriff more realistically, perhaps because Boone's strong presence kept him honest.

And best of all, the tourists were in a spending mood. Merchandise flowed out as quickly as shelves could be stocked.

Chelsea, demurely dressed as Rose's sister-in-law, Diana Taggart, climbed up on the wagon wheel and stepped over the box to take a seat beside Kit. She pushed back a few strands of hair that had escaped the chignon at her nape.

"I swear, women back then were crazy to put up with these clothes and hairstyles," she complained.

Muffled laughter from those in modern dress, gathered on the sidewalk, brought an answering smile to Kit's lips. "How you do go on," she said, a light warning to Chelsea to stay in character. "Do you think brother James will win with his Eastern racehorse?"

Chelsea tried to arrange her voluminous skirts more comfortably. "That horse came from my daddy's own stables, and it'll beat the pants—I mean the shoes—off any horse in the country."

"We'll see." Kit craned her neck, trying to peer around the slight bend in the street. "I happen to think that Sheriff Jack will—"

The crack of the starter's pistol, followed instantly by a roar from the crowd, cut off her words. Excitement shot though Kit and she jumped to her feet, eager to see which horse and rider would come around the bend first—Lee

Cox as James Taggart on a chestnut thoroughbred, or Bud as Sheriff Jack riding a rangy bay.

Neither, as it turned out. Boone and the big black Outlaw horse flashed hell-for-leather down the street and thundered toward the finish line. The cheers and exhortations of the crowd spurred him on.

Behind Boone, Lee and Bud raced neck and neck—but they raced for second place. The winner was never in doubt.

"Rats!" Chelsea exclaimed, watching the last of the competitors stream past. "I mean, fiddle-dee-dee!" Her cheeks were bright with excitement. "I thought sure my husband, James, would win."

"And I thought sure Sheriff Jack would win," Kit moaned. So much for victory kisses. "I suppose we should offer them consolation." She gathered her skirts in one hand, preparing to climb down from the buckboard—a tricky maneuver. "After all, it isn't if you win or lose, it's how you play the— Ummph!"

She'd backed into something; hampered by her clothing, trying to hang on to her parasol, she found herself clinging to the side of the buckboard unable to go up or down.

"Chelsea, help me!" she gasped, feeling her grip weakening.

It wasn't Chelsea who came to her rescue, but Boone. In fact, she soon realized, it was he who had stopped her descent; now he simply grabbed her around the waist and leapt onto the bed of the buckboard.

"What are you doing?" she cried, trying to reclaim her dignity and her balance. She shoved the tip of her umbrella into his chest. "How dare you touch me!"

A devilish grin tugged at Boone's mouth. "I've come to collect my prize," he said.

"What prize?"

"Doesn't the winner get a kiss?"

"From me? You must be joking!" She drew herself up haughtily.

"No, ma'am." He took a step toward her. "I'd never have entered the race if some cowboy hadn't told me that every year the winner gets a kiss from the prettiest gal in three counties. That gal, Miss Rose, has got to be you."

"But the sheriff was supposed to... I mean, Sheriff Jack *always* wins the race." She felt herself growing flustered. Bud-Jack was supposed to best this vicious gunman at every turn, including in the horse race. Where was the sheriff, anyway? She looked about wildly, searching the crowd.

"Not so fast."

She felt Boone's hands close over her upper arms, and before she could protest, he lifted Rose completely off her feet and kissed her.

And suddenly it was no longer Boone and Rose, it was Boone and Kit. Desperately she tried to push him away, all too aware of the power of his kiss to excite her.

The bed of the wagon tilted beneath her feet. Her eyes flew open—she didn't know when she'd closed them—and she saw Sheriff Jack, his face a mask of fury.

"I'll thank you to unhand the lady," he said, his voice threatening. "We don't cotton to strangers grabbin' good women in this town."

Carefully Boone stood Kit on her feet, made sure she had her balance before releasing her. There was something wickedly engaging about his grin. He turned toward Bud and the smile disappeared. "Just collectin' my winnings, Sheriff."

Tipping his hat to Kit, he leapt lightly to the ground. Sissy appeared out of nowhere, her feather boa ruffling in the breeze and her blowsy hair only barely contained. She wore red satin and black lace, somebody's idea of a Soiled Dove. She draped one arm around Boone's neck and gave Kit a scornful glance.

"Come on back to the Yellow Rose with me, sugar," she urged. "Anything you win there, you can damn sure collect!"

She planted a loud kiss on Boone's lips, winked at a middle-aged man in the crowd, patted a teenage boy on the fanny and sashayed away. Boone, and just about every other man in sight, followed her.

Only then did Kit glance around and realize that Bud was as nonplussed by what had happened as she was. She gave him a stunned look, which he returned.

"What's that guy up to?" he muttered, hitching up his belt. "He ain't playin' by the rules."

"He's trying to make up his own rules as he goes along," she said, giving her long skirts a vicious kick so she could climb down off the buckboard. "And I, for one, am having none of it!"

Wednesday, Day Four

KIT, ASSISTING RITA at an outdoor butter-churning exhibition, didn't see the fight on Main Street between James and Boone, but she knew it had started by the sudden exodus of her audience. Left alone, the two women looked at each other blankly, then laughed and relaxed.

"So, how's it going?" Rita asked, rotating her shoulders as if to relieve the strain. "Really, I mean."

Kit rolled her eyes. "Who knows? Boone seems to be heading in the opposite direction from the rest of us, doing his own thing."

Rita gave a slight nod. "Which makes a certain sort of sense, considering the Boone of legend."

"I suppose." Kit looked toward the sounds of crowd excitement. "Gosh, Rita, I'm really dreading this."

"What?"

Kit shuddered. "The scene that's coming up next—any scene with Boone. He keeps me so off balance that I don't know from minute to minute what I'm doing." She pulled a handkerchief from her cuff and mopped the back of her neck. "Well, he'd better not go too far, that's all I have to say! If he does I'll—"

The sound of running feet interrupted her, and she straightened, drawing in a deep breath to prepare for what came next. Mike Lopez skidded around the corner and came to a halt. At his heels raced at least two dozen excited people of all ages.

"Miz Rose, Miz Rose, come quick!"

"What is it, Mike? What's happened?"

"It's your brother, Miz Rose. That no-good gun-slingin' stranger has just beat the—"

"Michael!"

At the command in his mother's voice, the boy hauled in his enthusiasm. "He beat up your brother bad, Miz Rose! And it was the best fight anybody ever saw!"

He nodded vigorously and glanced around for support, which was forthcoming—"Better than TV," announced one youngster; "Awesome!" judged a second; and a panting middle-aged man chimed in, "Those guys are *good!*"

Kit didn't wait to hear any more. Brushing past the Greek chorus, she ran out into the street, casting about for the scene of battle.

She found it, in front of Curtis Mercantile and a horde of onlookers. Her "brother" sat in the dust, leaning back against a post and breathing hard. She ran to him, saw blood on his face and stopped short.

"My gosh, you're bleeding...." At the very last instant, she added, "James," instead of "Lee."

He looked up at her and groaned. "Stay out of this, will you, Rose? Just do me a favor and stay out of it."

Good—at least one member of the cast was following the script. "I can't stay out of it. You're my brother." She dropped to her knees beside him, tugging up the hem of her skirt to dab at his dusty bloody face—at least it looked like blood. And then *she* was the one who deviated from the script. "Good Lord, what did that beast do to you?"

Lee frowned. "Nothing I didn't try to do to him first," he ad-libbed. "I was takin' him to task for playin' fast and loose with you yesterday after the race. I guess I got more than I bargained for."

Gasping for breath, he struggled to his feet. Was he really hurt? Kit had no idea how much was real and how much was playacting—until Lee gave her a surreptitious wink. Which did little to calm her; she was good and mad at Boone for letting things get out of hand.

"Pardon me, pardon me, out of the way, please—I'm a doctor. Let me through, please."

The fascinated crowd parted reluctantly to let Doc Preston through. The doctor wore a neat black suit with white shirt and black string tie, and he carried a battered old medical bag that folks said once belonged to the town's first doctor.

"Hear you took a lickin'," Doc said cheerfully, leaning around to peer into Lee's face. "Can you walk? Good. Let's amble over to my office where I have all the tools of my trade in 1876 laid out, just in case anyone's curious."

Kit patted her "brother's" arm. "Yes, go with the doctor," she ordered. "I'll be along soon to see how you are."

"Wait a minute, sis." Lee-James grabbed her arm. "Where you goin'?"

Kit glanced toward the Yellow Rose. "Is he in there?" she demanded.

Numerous voices answered her: "Yes, you got it!"..."You bet!"..."Go get 'im, lady!"

"Don't go in there," James pleaded when he could be heard. "No decent woman would!"

Kit squared her shoulders and raised her chin. "Oh, no? Just watch me!"

Aware of the adrenaline flashing through her, she made no attempt to fight it down. She had many, many scores to settle with Boone Taggart, and she wasn't about to miss this chance.

CHAPTER TEN

KIT FLUNG OPEN the bat-wing doors and stepped into the Yellow Rose Saloon. It took a few seconds for her eyes to adjust to the dimness, and then she saw him, standing at the bar with one foot poised on the brass rail. He held a mug of beer halfway to his mouth.

An excited murmur coursed through the packed room. Only a few of those present were in costume; most were keen observers, not participants in the scene about to unfold. Kit didn't spare them a glance; all her attention was focused on the ruthless hard case at the bar.

She marched across the room, peanut shells crunching beneath her feet. She was supposed to launch into a tirade about his brutality; she was supposed to burst into tears; when he put his hands on her she was supposed to slap his face.

But now that the moment was here, words failed her. So Boone spoke first.

"Somebody better tell that brother of yours he can't afford to get mad until he gets big enough to whip somebody." He set his mug back on the shiny mahogany bar and straightened with lazy grace.

"You big bully! You hurt him!"

"He started it."

"That's a lie!"

A collective murmur ran through the audience. Boone's expression hardened and he gave "Rose" a faintly menacing smile. "If a *man* said that to me—"

"You'd do what?" Breathing hard, she ran with her anger. "I said it because it's true. Are you going to beat me up? Shoot me?" She crossed her arms and dared him to do his worst. "Go ahead, prove what a big brave man you are!"

"Yeah, I'm brave," he shot back. "Brave enough to handle *you.*"

Before she knew what he was doing, he dragged her into his arms and kissed her. She fought with everything she had, pressing the heels of her hands against his chest and aiming wild kicks at his shins.

Nevertheless, when he set her on her feet again, she knew she'd been well and truly kissed.

And when she reared back and let fly a roundhouse right to his jaw, he knew he'd been well and truly slapped.

The room erupted in pandemonium, which only increased with the entrance of the sheriff. Bud-Jack was followed by a swarm of people who'd been trying to watch through the windows and now saw their chance to squeeze inside.

The press of bodies shoved Kit against Boone. He caught her in his arms and turned around, protecting her with his body.

Leaning down, he yelled in her ear, "I'll shoot that damned sheriff before I'll let you marry him—or any other man!"

"That's not in the script!" Kit shouted back. She banged her clenched fists against his chest. "The sheriff's supposed to back you down like the yellow dog you are!"

Holding her pinned against the bar, he cupped her face with his hands. "To hell with the script—nobody can hear us now, anyway. I think I'd better get you out of this crush before you get hurt."

Planting a quick kiss on her astonished lips, he picked her up in his arms and elbowed his way toward the rear exit. Behind them, the sheriff roared for order.

Thursday, Day Five

DUB PARTRIDGE and his two boys rode into town Thursday afternoon, and they certainly looked the part of no-good outlaws. Dusty and unshaven, shabbily dressed and heavily armed, they tied their horses at the saloon hitching post and went inside.

Boone wasn't in sight. Later that day when he passed them on the street, he gave them little more than a glance.

"What's going on?" Kit complained to Rita while they pretended to shop at Curtis Mercantile. "Boone's supposed to be thick as thieves with the Partridges."

"Don't ask," Rita said through gritted teeth. She put down the reel of ribbon she'd been examining. "Okay, it's time. Go get proposed to, Miss Rose."

So Kit did. Bud was loitering outside just the way he was supposed to be, and this time he stuck to the script. Sheriff Jack proposed, Miss Rose accepted, and the audience applauded. The scene went without a hitch—right up until the final minutes.

The sheriff had departed and Kit had turned to walk back to the hotel when Boone appeared—which he wasn't supposed to do. She gave him a dirty look, lifted her chin to a regal angle and tried to sweep past. He stepped into her path, pulling his hat from his head.

He looked her in the eye without smiling. "I meant what I said yesterday in the Yellow Rose," he said. "Don't make me prove it."

Leaving her with mouth agape, he sauntered off.

That night, the Fourth of July was celebrated with a stupendous fireworks display. Watching, Kit felt the knot of tension inside her grow tighter and tighter.

She could almost understand why young men ran and rode through the streets firing off blanks and yelling at the tops of their lungs. She could almost envy them, she thought, turning to enter the hotel.

Then she stopped short. Boone was leaning against a post watching her, the strong planes of his face illuminated by the "rocket's red glare." He tipped his hat.

"Evenin', Miss Rose. You are truly a sight for sore eyes."

His slow sweet voice rolled right down her spine, making her shiver. Swallowing hard, she turned her back on him and hurried inside.

Friday, Day Six

THE FRIDAY-NIGHT barn dance was the hottest ticket in town. Even with all the corrals of the old livery stable transformed and opened up for dancing, as well as the street, there wasn't room for everyone who wanted to attend.

Kit didn't share the prevailing eagerness. Although things appeared to be going swimmingly, it was only surface deep. Sheriff Jack grew more and more moody; Kit grew more and more confused; and Boone…well, Boone was looking more and more pleased with himself.

When he grabbed her hand and swung her onto the dance floor, Kit looked around frantically for the sheriff.

"Will you *please* leave me alone?" she demanded, trying to hold herself stiff and apart.

"Nope." He hauled her hard against him.

"But I'm an engaged woman!" she cried breathlessly.

"You'll never marry him."

"I will! The sheriff is a fine man."

"But you don't love him. You love me, or you will, once you start bein' honest with yourself."

"You're crazy! You can't just come riding into town and expect to take over—"

"I'm cuttin' in."

At the sound of the rough male voice, Kit thought deliverance was at hand. But it was only Shayne Partridge, looking extraordinarily loutish. Standing nearby, his identical twin brother, Dwayne, looked . . . identical.

Shayne grabbed Kit's arm and tried to haul her away from Boone; Boone, his arm around her waist, resisted. Kit, the object of this tug-of-war, felt the breath whoosh from her lungs. She sensed other dancers and onlookers drawing back to clear a space around the four of them.

Dwayne, who had been watching, grinned and dropped into a crouch. His arms curved out from his sides and his hands hovered above the butts of his pistols. "Want me to shoot him?" he asked eagerly, darting a glance at his twin.

Kit spoke without thinking. "I wish you would." She twisted away, breaking free of both Shayne and Boone. She was breathing hard and was completely confused; she had never rehearsed any such scene as the one unfolding. "In fact," she continued, voice rising, "I wish you'd shoot each *other.* I don't know what's going on here, but I won't be a party—"

Dwayne went for his gun and Kit screamed—she couldn't help it. He pulled the weapon from his holster

and suddenly his wolfish expression gave way to disbelief. Glancing around, Kit saw that Boone's revolver was
already up and pointed, his finger beginning to squeeze
the trigger—

"Oh, no! Stop!"

She forgot this was all a game of make-believe and
threw herself forward at the same moment Dub Partridge called out to his boys, "You, Dwayne! Shayne, take
that weapon away from your brother before he gets his-
self shot. You boys get outta here while the gettin's good."

Boone's smile came slow and satisfied. With an elabo-
rate twirl, he returned his pistol to its holster. "No need
to worry about me, Miz Rose. I can take care of myself
and you, too."

"Oh!" She lifted her right arm, prepared to deliver a
stinging blow, but he caught her wrist and held it still. His
eyes laughed at her.

"You'll have to learn better manners after we're married," he drawled. "Wouldn't want the kids pickin' up
bad habits."

"Married! I wouldn't marry you if you were the last
man on earth, Boone...." She'd almost said "Boone
Taggart." She yanked her arm away and rubbed at her
wrist where his fingers had left marks, struggling to get
her bearings again. The Boone of history had no last
name; he was always simply Boone, the Mysterious Gunfighter.

But now Boone responded, "Smith. The name's Boone
Smith. Remember it, because it's going to be yours one
day."

Tipping his hat, he turned and left her standing there
alone on the dance floor to enthusiastic applause. That's
where Sheriff Jack found her a minute later.

He muttered some excuse about breaking up a fight outside, but after what she'd been through, Kit was in no mood to make allowances.

Saturday, Day Seven

LIFTING THE HEM of Diana Taggart's beautiful Victorian wedding gown, Kit paced the floor of the small room behind the altar of the little church on the hill at the end of Main Street. She'd begun this final round of events with trepidation. Showdown Days was out of control, and she simply didn't know what to expect next.

With hands that shook, she smoothed the Brussels lace at the front of the ivory satin gown. A tulle veil, secured with a cluster of orange blossoms just above the pompadour roll of her hair, flowed down her back and the entire length of the train. Long-sleeved, high-necked and tightly fitted, the gown with its accompanying corset made normal breathing impossible.

Chelsea rushed in. "He's coming," she gasped, pressing one hand to her chest as if that would help her get her breath. "Lord, I don't know how women could stand wearing this stuff!"

"The sheriff is coming?"

Chelsea looked startled. "Of course—who else? Let me straighten your train and you can come outside to watch."

Kit hardly noticed the pews filled with curious observers, or heard their gasps of appreciation as she hurried down the aisle and out onto the small porch. Shading her eyes, she looked toward Main Street.

She could see Sheriff Jack, walking down the middle of the street in his black broadcloth suit and white shirt. The three Partridges loitered in front of the saloon, and they looked threatening even at this distance. As the sheriff drew even with them, the three tough hombres stepped into the street.

Kit's heart leapt with dread and maybe a little fear. Now Boone would show his true colors and reveal himself as the leader of this little band of desperadoes.

But the Partridges didn't wait—they were about to go for their guns. She saw Bud draw aside his coattails to show he wasn't even wearing a gun belt, and she uttered a small cry of alarm. Was he crazy? He couldn't possibly have forgotten.

She started down the stairs, hardly aware of what she was doing. This no longer seemed like a game, an entertainment cooked up for the benefit of tourists. It was beginning to feel all too real, and her attention centered on the tableau unfolding in the street below.

Boone stepped out of Curtis Mercantile across the way, and Kit gasped in relief, hoping everything was back on track. But that was impossible; without a gun how could the sheriff shoot the lot of them?

She saw Boone crouch; he held something in his hand, something he tossed to the sheriff—a revolver, spinning through the air in a graceful glittering arc. With the same economical movement, Boone drew his own weapon and . . .

Kit grabbed her gown in both hands and raced down the hill toward the action. Her heavy train dragged in the dust; her veil streamed out behind her but didn't slow her mad dash. Boone wasn't supposed to help the sheriff. He was supposed to wait until Rose got close and then grab her to use as a hostage—

But six-guns blazed; two of the Partridges recoiled, as if from the impact of bullets, and went down. The third— Shayne, she thought, but couldn't be sure—executed a spectacular flying leap onto the back of a handy horse and thundered out of town, escorted by the wild cheers of spectators lining the street.

The sheriff reeled against a hitching post in front of the general store, holding his arm and glaring at the onlookers. Pounding to a halt, Kit whirled to confront Boone. "Of all the low-down, back-stabbing, double-dealing coyotes!"

"That temper's gonna get you in a peck of trouble one of these days, Miss Rose." Boone untied the powerful Outlaw horse from the saloon rail and swung up into the saddle.

"You've ruined everything!" she raved, flinging herself at him. The Outlaw danced aside, and she grabbed the saddle strings and hung on.

"No, I haven't," Boone said calmly. Leaning down, he caught her beneath the arms and scooped her up in front of him in the saddle. "I've set the record straight, Miss Kitty-Rose Taggart."

Holding her tight so she couldn't fall, he pulled her back into the cradle of his arms and kissed her breathless. Then he kicked the Outlaw into a gallop and they raced out of town.

The tourists loved it.

THIS TIME he'd really gone too far. Kit's anger expanded with every passing mile, and she held herself tense and aloof in front of him. It wasn't enough he'd ruined her life and Thom T.'s life. Now he threatened the economic well-being of every man, woman and child in Showdown, Texas, with his childish shenanigans.

She would never forgive him for this, never!

A few miles out of town, Boone turned off the road and pointed the stallion cross-county at a gentle lope. He did not, however, ease the pressure of his arms around Kit.

"You mad?" he asked after a while.

"Mad? Mad? Why should I be mad!" Angry words she'd been fighting to contain burst forth. Twisting so she could see his face, she demanded, "Why did you do it, Boone? Why did you mess with history and ruin Showdown Days?"

He regarded her warily. "I didn't mess with history, Kitty. I corrected it. Temporarily, anyway."

"Give me a break!" She tried to push away from him, which was, of course, impossible, balanced as she was on the pommel with one knee hooked around the saddle horn. In fact, she sat more on Boone than anywhere else—and she didn't like it one bit. "Let me down," she commanded. "Right now!"

"But Kit, we're miles from anywhere—"

"I don't care if we're stranded on the moon! Let me off this horse this minute or I'll—"

"I know," he said dryly, "Or else you'll never forgive me." He pulled in the Outlaw and, without dismounting himself, let her slide down the animal's side onto her feet.

She staggered erect, surprised at how wobbly her knees felt. With shaky hands she smoothed the wedding gown around her and took a deep breath. Perspiration trickled down her back and between her breasts; a blazing sun seemed to pierce the layers of fabric with ease.

Boone crossed his hands on the saddle horn, reins grasped loosely, and waited.

She lifted her chin defiantly. "Well, what are you looking at? Why don't you just—" she flapped one hand in a dismissive gesture "—go away?"

"Not a chance," he said. "You're going to listen to me, whether you want to or not."

"Ohhh!" She stamped one granny-booted foot in the dust. She felt her face flame, whether with heat or anger or both she had no way of knowing. "You're nothing but a . . . a bully!" Tossing the bedraggled bridal veil over her shoulder, she picked up her skirts and turned back toward town, the long train dragging behind her.

Boone nudged the black stallion forward. "Hey, you're going the wrong way. Rocking T's the other direction."

"I'm not going to the ranch. I'm going back to Showdown to salvage anything I can from this mess. If the sheriff hasn't turned in his badge, maybe we can still—"

"Kit, Thom T.'s at the ranch and he's got something to tell you."

She stopped short, so short that the Outlaw stepped on her train and bumped her between the shoulder blades with his muzzle. She took a stumbling step forward while the horse shied to one side. Catching her balance, she whirled on her tormentors.

"It's not enough that you harass me, now you've sicced your horse on me!"

Outlaw snorted and danced away, bowing his neck. Boone settled him with a few words. "I deny everything and so does he." He straightened in the saddle, suddenly speaking impatiently. "Look, if you really want to go back to town I'll take you. But even if you don't owe me a hearing, don't you think you owe one to Thom T.?"

"*Owe* one?" Maybe so, but if she went, it would be because she loved the old man as much as she detested his grandson. *When* she went . . .

Without another word she lifted her right arm toward Boone; he clasped it, forearm to forearm, wrist to elbow. Throwing her train over one shoulder, she let him swing her up behind him. At least this was better than sitting on his lap, she thought as she settled on the saddle skirt.

But she'd be darned if she'd put her arms around his waist. Grasping the curve of the cantle with both hands, she announced, "I'm ready. Let's get this over with."

And as they rode along, he told her another version of the legend of Showdown as revealed in Taggart correspondence and memorabilia. At first she tried not to listen, but that was impossible, because she *did* want to know, she *did* care, and it was foolish to try to tell herself otherwise.

The details, Boone said, had come to light last year when Thom T. hired a private detective to find out once and for all if Rose had any living descendants.

Kit stiffened. "Smith. You said your name was Boone Smith—in the play, I mean. And last winter I came to the wedding of Trey Smith, introduced by your grandpa as a long-lost—" she frowned "—cousin or something."

"'Or something' is right," Boone agreed. "Trey's great-great-grandmother was Rose Taggart, and his great-great-grandfather was Boone, the Mysterious Gunfighter, real name, Boone Smith."

Kit felt faint. "Then Rose didn't love the sheriff?"

"She loved the gunman and eloped with him after the gunfight—yes, there really was a gunfight, but the gunman and the sheriff were on the same side. We're not sure who they were fighting or why, because they really were rivals for Rose's affections, but when the dust cleared, all three of them left town. It's come down in the legend that Rose went with Jack, but she didn't—she went with Boone."

"Then ... who's buried in Boone's grave behind the church?" Kit wanted to know. "Was Boone an outlaw? What became of Sheriff Jack?"

"I can't answer all those questions," Boone admitted. "I can tell you that Boone Smith and Rose completely separated themselves from the family and Jones, Texas, apparently to escape his reputation. He even went so far as to stop using the name Boone, which was one of the reasons it was so hard to trace them. His full name was Jeremy Edward Boone Smith, and he started going by his initials—J.E.B., for Jeb.''

''That was the price Rose paid—to leave her home and family for the man she loved,'' Kit said with a catch in her voice. It was such a beautiful story she almost felt like crying. ''I guess it makes a sort of strange sense,'' she admitted grudgingly. ''I never quite believed that story about Diana having Boones in her family tree.'' But then doubts surfaced once more. ''If this is true, why wasn't I told? I met Trey Smith and I've known Rachel ever since I came here—I was at their wedding, for goodness' sake!''

Boone shrugged, the movement catching her unawares and bringing them into momentary contact. She caught her breath and sat very still on the Outlaw's broad rump. Boone turned the big horse through the gated entrance to the ranch before answering.

''Better still,'' he countered, ''why wasn't I told? I think Meg and Jesse intended to tell me just before they left, but I... Never mind that, the bottom line is I *didn't* know. When Thom T. let me in on it he explained that all concerned had decided the fewer who knew the better, since the consequences for the town were so potentially dire.''

''That's for sure.'' She frowned. ''What made him tell you now? What made you come back here and turn Showdown Days into a shambles? What could have been so important—''

He interrupted with a single word: ''You.''

''M-me?''

''You. And the fact that I . . .''

She felt his tension and for a moment thought he wouldn't go on.

" . . . love you."

"You love me?" When had she slipped her arms around his lean waist? When had she leaned forward to press her cheek against his taut back? Too late to worry about that now.

"Damn," he swore, "this isn't easy. I'm a man who takes great pride in self-control, and yet here I am, playing dress-up and practically kidnapping you—and me an officer of the court."

"You love me?" she repeated wonderingly.

"I said I did, didn't I? Now the question is, how do you feel about me? Are you still going to hate me forever, or can we work out something a little more . . . agreeable?"

"Agreeable?" Her temper flared. There was only one "something" in which she had the slightest interest, and it was called marriage. If he had anything else in mind . .

"You're beginning to sound like a parrot," he snapped. "Look, I feel silly enough riding along dressed like a gunslinger with a kidnapped bride bouncing along behind—"

"I don't bounce!" She tightened her arms around him until her breasts pressed hard against his back. Her heart pounded so wildly she could barely breathe.

Boone drew in the big black horse in front of the ranch house. Throwing his right leg over the saddle horn, he slid down and out of her embrace. Then he held out his arms to her, and she slipped into them without the slightest hesitation.

He cupped her hands between his and stared into her eyes. "There's something I've got to know before you talk to Thom T.," he said.

Her mouth went dry. "W-what?"

He drew in a quick breath. "You said it yourself—Rose gave up everything to be with the man she loved. Would you . . . will you do the same?"

She couldn't have answered if her life depended on it. Stunned and disbelieving, she stared at him.

"Kit, I'm asking if you love me." His hungry glance devoured her. "No, I take that back," he amended fiercely. "I *know* you love me. I'm just not sure you love me enough."

Now was not the time for hyperbole, Kit realized; now was the time for naked truth. So she gave it to him. "Daniel Boone Taggart, I fell in love with you when I was fifteen years old!"

He frowned. "I'm talking about now. I'm asking how you feel today—right this minute." He slid his hands up her satin-covered arms until he could grasp her shoulders. "I said I love you, Kitty McCrae, and I meant it. Now the only question is, do you love me? Will you marry me and go with me wherever fate takes us? Do I rate ahead of the Rocking T, or behind it?"

She licked her lips. "That's three questions."

"See what you do to me? I can't even count!"

"Oh, Boone . . ." She stared him straight in the eye. "Yes. Yes to everything. I love you, I'll marry you, and you rate ahead of the Rocking T. But I'll never stop trying to get you to—"

He didn't wait to hear what she would never stop; he kissed her. And deep in her heart, delirious joy mingled with bittersweet regret that, although he might love her a tiny fraction as much as she loved him, nothing else had really changed.

The ranch would still be gone, and the civilized East would still fence in old Thom T. something awful. But she would never stop trying to convince Boone to see her point of view, and maybe with enough time and love, he would come to realize—

"Gol dang it, it's about time yawl got home. You young 'uns plan to keep that up all day, or yawl comin' inside?"

Kit twisted in Boone's arms. Thom T. stood on the porch, wearing a big smile and no leg cast. *Home,* he'd said. New hope fluttered in Kit's breast, and she looked questioningly at Boone.

"The Rocking T won't be sold," he told her gently, giving her the most beautiful smile she'd ever seen. "You were right, Kit. I did lose sight of my grandfather's feelings. Thom T.'s back to stay, but I didn't want that to influence you."

"In-influence me?"

"Influence your answer." He stroked her cheek, his expression more vulnerable than she'd ever seen it. "Honey, you were right about everything—Thom T. would never be happy anywhere but here. Even he forgot that for a little while. Thank God, you didn't."

She pressed her palms to her cheeks. "I'm confused— everything's happening so fast. Are you saying . . . ?"

"I'm saying when we got back East I sat down and analyzed the situation. That's when I concluded that I love you. I also faced the undeniable fact that I love this piece of Texas dirt, and I love that old man standing there grinning at us fit to bust. I'm saying I didn't know what happy was until Thom T. called me home a few weeks ago and I found you here, grown-up and waiting for me."

"Oh, Boone! Why did it take you so long to realize all this?" Kit threw herself into his arms. All her dreams seemed suddenly to be coming true. Now if only . . .

And then he said the words that completed the circle of her happiness. "Kit, there'll be Taggarts running this ranch for a long time to come—and lots of little Taggarts growing up to love the Rocking T as much as we do. I can practice law in Texas. I don't have to live in New York or London to be happy. Hell, I *wasn't* happy."

He pressed swift kisses to her cheek, her eyelids, her trembling lips. "But now," he said with satisfaction so deep she could feel it, "*now* I'm happy."

EPILOGUE

WELL-WISHERS OVERFLOWED the little church on the hill at the end of Main Street the day Kit McCrae married Daniel Boone Taggart. Jesse and Meg Taggart, the groom's brother and sister-in-law, sat in the first pew beside Trey and Rachel Smith—"He's Boone and Jesse's third cousin, twice removed," Jenny Merton confided solemnly to her niece, Chelsea.

Since the Merton women sat in the last pew and since Thom T. was loitering in the back of the church, the old man overheard Jenny's comment and barely managed to stifle a gleeful snort. Dang few knew the truth about the Taggarts, and that was the way he wanted to keep it. The entire town seemed convinced that Boone's eccentric version of Showdown Days was nothing more than a young man's prank, better forgotten.

Thom T., for one, had no intention of disabusing anyone of that notion. What they didn't know wouldn't hurt them.

Waiting to escort the bride to the flower-bedecked altar and the tall tuxedoed man who would claim her as his own, Thom T. rubbed his hands together with satisfaction. How he loved a happy ending! He beamed at Rachel's teenaged son, Jason, serving as an usher along with Meg and Jesse's eight-year-old Randy.

Both boys were doing their best to appear solemn and dignified, but when they caught Thom T. looking at them, they couldn't resist devilish grins in response. Good boys, both of them, the old man thought. Some day...

The first strains of the wedding march, as played by Dixie Baker, sounded. Kit and Boone had chosen a traditional wedding service, agreeing that was best for such an old-fashioned couple. Boone had teased her, saying "old-fashioned" simply meant she'd insisted they have the wedding before the honeymoon.

"That way you have something to look forward to," she'd shot back, then glanced at Thom T. with a mortified blush on her cheeks. Which apparently hadn't bothered Boone one bit; he'd put his arms around her and showed her with a kiss that she, too, had plenty to anticipate—with his grandfather's delighted approval.

Thom T. sighed. Things couldn't have turned out better all around if he'd planned it—which he had.

Waiting for the bride, he glanced through the open door and saw the erect and dignified figure of John Hayslip Randall IV hurrying up the steps. Thom T. pulled out his pocket watch and checked the time. Meg's stuffed-shirt Boston grandpa didn't like being late, and he very nearly was this time.

Reaching the door, the seventy-something Randall stepped inside and offered his hand. "Taggart," he said somewhat breathlessly.

"Randall." The eighty-something Taggart shook his hand.

The two old men, natural enemies by birth and circumstance, eyed each other warily. Then smiles seemed to creep up on both simultaneously.

John shook his head as if in amazement. "Meg is absolutely correct in her assessment of you," he said in that formal way of his that had rankled so on other occasions. "You, sir, are a scalawag."

This time his formality struck Thom T. as more amusing than irritating. "Wouldn't doubt it a bit," he acquiesced cheerfully.

"Would you really have done it?"

"Done what?"

"Sold that benighted parcel of real estate you pioneers call a ranch."

"Not only no," Thom T. declared, "but *hell* no. Fortunately you and me's the only ones seem to know that, huh, Johnny?"

Again they exchanged smiles.

Randy, the great-grandson they shared, tugged at John's sleeve. "Great-grandpa John? Come sit down. I think it's about to start."

"Right you are, Randall." John patted the boy absently on top of the head, still looking at Thom T. "I honestly don't know how you coaxed young Daniel Boone to give up a flourishing law career in New York and return to this backwater, Taggart, but... congratulations."

Thom T. cocked his head to one side. "Ain't no hill for a stepper," he announced without a shred of false modesty. "The hard part was lettin' that dang sissy horse throw me and break my laig!"

AND SO WHEN Kit appeared, looking more radiantly lovely in the Taggart-family wedding gown than any woman had a right to look, Thom T. proudly escorted her down the aisle. Past beaming faces they walked with measured steps, Rita following demurely as matron of honor.

At the altar, Thom T. lifted Kit's veil and kissed away the tears of happiness dampening her cheeks. Placing her hand in Boone's, the old man stepped back to take his place as his grandson's best man.

The minister began to speak. "Dearly beloved, we are gathered here today in the sight of God and this company...."

Thom T. let out a sigh of pure contentment. If ever a man had reason to be grateful...

The sound of shuffling feet caught his attention. Glancing from the corner of his eye, he saw Randy, seated next to his other great-grandfather. The boy looked bored and restless, as well a lad his age might at the mushiness of the proceedings. Looking at the youngest of his line, Thom T. began to smile.

I've got a few good years left in me, he thought. *Maybe when Randy's full growed...*

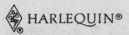

HARLEQUIN®

my Valentine

1993

The most romantic day of the year is here! Escape into the exquisite world of love with MY VALENTINE 1993. What better way to celebrate Valentine's Day than with this very romantic, sensuous collection of four original short stories, written by some of Harlequin's most popular authors.

**ANNE STUART
JUDITH ARNOLD
ANNE McALLISTER
LINDA RANDALL WISDOM**

THIS VALENTINE'S DAY, DISCOVER ROMANCE WITH MY VALENTINE 1993

Available in February wherever Harlequin Books are sold.   VAL93

COME FOR A VISIT—TEXAS-STYLE!

Where do you find hot Texas nights, smooth Texas charm and dangerously sexy cowboys? CRYSTAL CREEK!

This March, join us for a year in Crystal Creek...where power and influence live in the land, and in the hands of one family determined to nourish old Texas fortunes and to forge new Texas futures.

CRYSTAL CREEK reverberates with the exciting rhythm of Texas. Each story features the rugged individuals who live and love in the Lone Star State. And each one ends with the same invitation...

Y'ALL COME BACK...REAL SOON!

Watch for this exciting saga of a unique Texas family in March, wherever Harlequin Books are sold.

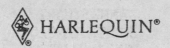

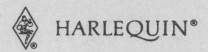 **HARLEQUIN®**

THE TAGGARTS OF TEXAS!

Harlequin's Ruth Jean Dale brings you
THE TAGGARTS OF TEXAS!

Those Taggart men—strong, sexy and hard to resist...

You've met Jesse James Taggart in FIREWORKS!
Harlequin Romance #3205 (July 1992)

And Trey Smith—he's THE RED-BLOODED YANKEE!
Harlequin Temptation #413 (October 1992)

Now meet Daniel Boone Taggart in SHOWDOWN!
Harlequin Romance #3242 (January 1993)

And finally the Taggarts who started it all—in LEGEND!
Harlequin Historical #168 (April 1993)

Read all the Taggart romances!
Meet all the Taggart men!

Available wherever Harlequin Books are sold.

ROMANCE IS A YEARLONG EVENT!

Celebrate the most romantic day of the year with MY VALENTINE! (February)

CRYSTAL CREEK
When you come for a visit Texas-style, you won't want to leave! (March)

Celebrate the joy, excitement and adjustment that comes with being JUST MARRIED! (April)

Go back in time and discover the West as it was meant to be . . . UNTAMED— Maverick Hearts! (July)

LINGERING SHADOWS
New York Times bestselling author Penny Jordan brings you her latest blockbuster. Don't miss it! (August)

BACK BY POPULAR DEMAND!!!
Calloway Corners, involving stories of four sisters coping with family, business and romance! (September)

FRIENDS, FAMILIES, LOVERS
Join us for these heartwarming love stories that evoke memories of family and friends. (October)

Capture the magic and romance of Christmas past with HARLEQUIN HISTORICAL CHRISTMAS STORIES! (November)

WATCH FOR FURTHER DETAILS IN ALL HARLEQUIN BOOKS!

CALEND